UNINVITED GUESTS

Grandmother looked around. "Please explain what's going on," she said in a weary voice. "If you can, that is."

"You were in Corey's room last night," I said. "You saw what we saw, you heard what we heard. I wish we could explain it, but . . ." I shrugged, unable to think of anything else to say.

Grandmother removed the chair from the desk, set it on the floor, and, with a sigh, sat on it. Shutting her eyes, she took a deep breath. "That's right. I saw, and I heard. As a result, I lay awake for hours trying to think of an explanation. And failed. Utterly."

Rising to her feet, Grandmother said, "I suggest we have breakfast. After that, please clean up your room. When everything is back to normal, I'd like to pretend last night did not happen."

Turning my back on the wreckage, I followed Grandmother to the dining room. She could chase off the psychics, she could make me clean up my room, she could pretend last night hadn't happened—she could even send Corey and me back to New York—but the ghosts were here, and they weren't leaving.

Not until they got what they wanted . . . whatever that was.

Other novels by
MARY DOWNING HAHN

Closed for the Season
Deep and Dark and Dangerous
Witch Catcher
The Old Willis Place
Hear the Wind Blow
Anna on the Farm
Promises to the Dead
Anna All Year Round
As Ever, Gordy
The Gentleman Outlaw and Me—Eli
Look for Me by Moonlight
Time for Andrew
The Wind Blows Backward
Stepping on the Cracks
The Dead Man in Indian Creek
The Doll in the Garden
Tallahassee Higgins
Wait Till Helen Comes
Daphne's Book

MARY DOWNING HAHN

ALL
THE
LOVELY
BAD
ONES

sandpiper

Houghton Mifflin Harcourt
Boston   New York

The poem from which the title of this book is taken was written in 1885 by James Whitcomb Riley (1849–1916). It is popularly known as "Little Orphant Annie," but its original title was "The Elf-Child."

The text of this book is set in Aldus Roman.

www.sandpiperbooks.com

The Library of Congress has cataloged the hardcover edition as follows:

Hahn, Mary Downing.
All the lovely bad ones: a ghost story / by Mary Downing Hahn.
p. cm.
Summary: While spending the summer at their grandmother's Vermont inn, two prankster siblings awaken young ghosts from the inn's distant past who refuse to "rest in peace."

[1. Ghosts—Fiction. 2. Haunted houses—Fiction. 3. Brothers and sisters—Fiction. 4. Hotels, motels, etc.—Fiction. 5. Behavior—Fiction. 6. Vermont—Fiction.] I. Title.

PZ7.H1256Al 2008
[Fic]—dc22

2007037932

ISBN: 978-0-618-85467-7
ISBN: 978-0-547-24878-3 pb

Manufactured in the United States of America

DOM 10 9 8 7 6 5 4 3 2 1

To all the little children: —The happy ones; and sad ones;
The sober and the silent ones; the boisterous and glad ones;
The good ones—Yes, the good ones, too; and all the lovely bad ones.

—James Whitcomb Riley,
dedication to "Little Orphant Annie"

1

Grandmother met us at the Burlington airport, a big smile on her face and her arms open for a hug. With a squeal of delight, my sister rushed toward her, but I held back. Public displays of affection were okay for girls, I guessed, but not for guys. After all, I'd be thirteen soon—way too old for that kind of silly stuff.

After giving Corey a big hug, Grandmother turned to me. "Just look at you, Travis. You've shot up since Christmas. How tall are you?"

I shrugged. "About five six, maybe seven. Not all that tall. There's a guy in my class who's already six feet."

"I'm almost as tall as Travis," Corey put in, never one to be left out. "And I'm a whole year younger."

While Corey chattered about the plane ride from New York, Grandmother led us to the baggage claim. We grabbed our suitcases and headed for the parking lot. The late-afternoon air was cool and the sky was blue, a change from the heat and humidity we'd left in the city.

"Welcome to Vermont." Grandmother opened the door of a shiny red pickup truck. "Toss your luggage in the back and climb aboard."

Corey jumped in beside Grandmother, and I squeezed in by the door.

"So do you think you'll be able to stand being away

from your parents for a whole summer?" Grandmother asked.

My sister and I looked at each other and grinned. "We'll miss them a little," Corey said, "but we're used to summers away from home."

Grandmother smiled. "I'm glad you chose the inn instead of camp."

Corey and I didn't look at each for fear we'd laugh and give ourselves away. We hadn't had a choice, actually. Camp Willow Tree had made it very clear that neither Corey nor I was welcome to return. It seemed we'd failed to get into the true spirit of camp. We'd started food fights, played hooky from evening campfire, made up rude words to the camp song, overturned a canoe on purpose, and let the air out of a counselor's bike tires the day we were supposed to ride twenty miles up a mountain in the pouring rain. Was it our fault the camp staff had no sense of humor?

The truth of it was Corey and I tended to get in trouble wherever we went. Bad ones—that's what we were. Well, not really *bad*. We preferred to think of ourselves as pranksters. But like the camp staff, adults (including Mom and Dad) didn't find our antics as funny as we did.

Our parents had made us promise to behave ourselves at the inn. One bad report from Grandmother and we'd spend the rest of our vacation taking pre-algebra in summer school—a fate even worse than camp craft projects involving Popsicle sticks and feathers.

Just before the turnoff for Middlebury, we left Route 7 and took a winding road that rolled over hills, past farms and fields, red barns and sturdy farmhouses. Herds of black and white cows raised their heads to watch us go by. Beyond them, the mountains rose greenish blue against the sky.

"Here we are." Grandmother pointed to a neatly painted sign: THE INN AT FOX HILL—NEXT RIGHT. Under the words was a picture of a smiling fox. A VACANCY sign hung below.

Grandmother swung into a long, straight driveway shaded by tall trees. At its end was a three-story pink brick building. The late-afternoon sun touched everything with gold—the lawn, flower beds, and wooden rocking chairs on the front porch. Behind the inn, clouds cast their shadows on the Green Mountains.

Grandmother parked the truck, and Corey and I jumped out. I grabbed for my suitcase, but Grandmother said, "Leave your luggage for now. Henry can bring it in later. Martha's promised to have a pitcher of ice-cold lemonade, freshly squeezed, and a plateful of chocolate-chip cookies, still warm from the oven."

We followed Grandmother down a stone path bordered with dense white flowers to a brick patio shaded by a huge wisteria climbing over a trellis. Nearby, a fountain splashed into a pool, and I glimpsed flashes of red fish swimming in its depths. Flowers bloomed everywhere, and bees hummed. Birds called back and forth in the trees.

As we settled ourselves around a table, a woman strode toward us carrying a tray. Her gray hair was pulled back tightly into a knot, and her mouth seemed to have settled into a permanent frown. Without so much as a smile, she set the tray down and stepped back.

"Thank you, Martha. It looks lovely." Gesturing to Corey and me, Grandmother introduced us to the woman.

"Pleased to meet you." Still no smile, just a quick dip of the head.

"Mrs. Brewster is our cook," Grandmother told us. "People come to the inn year after year just to eat her famous blueberry pie."

Another dip of the head and Mrs. Brewster left us to enjoy the lemonade and cookies.

"Martha's a little standoffish," Grandmother admitted, "but she and her husband more or less came with the inn. And she's truly magnificent in the kitchen."

Corey jabbed my ankle with the toe of her shoe and whispered, "She looks like an old grump to me."

Grandmother leaned across the table to brush a strand of hair out of Corey's eyes. "You'll change your mind when you eat your first meal here."

Corey helped herself to a cookie. While she chewed, she looked around. "Is that a swimming pool?"

Grandmother nodded. "You can use it any time you like—as long as someone's with you. I don't have a lifeguard."

She pointed past the pool to the wide grassy lawn, dotted with old-fashioned Adirondack chairs, turned to face the mountains. "If you like tennis, the court's over there. I have bicycles for the guests. The state park just down the road has a great network of biking and hiking trails."

Grandmother ate a cookie. "If it rains," she went on, "there's a library, computer, TV, DVD player, and at least a dozen old-fashioned board games. Hopefully, you'll find plenty to do."

Corey and I leaned back in our chairs and drank our lemonade, just as fresh and cold as Grandmother had promised. It looked as if it was going to be a good summer. No schedules. No organized activities. Nobody blowing whistles at us. No boring crafts. For once, we were free to do what we wanted to do. Including nothing. Nothing at all.

Corey studied the inn. "Do you have many guests?"

"There are six rooms," Grandmother said. "Four on the second floor and two on the third. We can house twelve guests, but tonight we only have two—a couple of young men."

Corey looked around. "Where are they?"

"They've gone out bicycling, but they'll be back soon for dinner."

"You must usually have more people than that," Corey said.

Grandmother sighed. "That's what I thought when I bought the place, but the inn's kind of remote. Tourists like to be closer to Burlington or Middlebury, Stowe or Woodstock." She shifted in her chair as if she were about to get up but then changed her mind.

"Actually, the inn's location is only part of the problem," she added slowly.

Corey and I sat up straighter, as if we both sensed something exciting.

For a moment, Grandmother stared at the inn, her gaze drifting from one window to the next as if she were admiring the flower boxes.

"I wouldn't bother telling you," she said at last, "but you're sure to hear the guests talking about it. Fox Hill is mentioned in *Haunted Inns of Vermont*."

Corey and I leaned closer, our eyes wide. A little shiver raced up and down my spine. A whole summer in a haunted inn—what could be more exciting than that?

"Oooh," Corey murmured. "I've always wanted to see a ghost."

"Don't be stupid," I told her. "You can't even watch a horror movie without having nightmares."

"Huh," Corey said. "Just last week I watched one of the *Scream* movies, and I didn't even close my eyes or cover my ears once!"

"Don't worry." Grandmother patted Corey's hand. "No one has seen a ghost since the Cornells sold the inn to me."

"Where do you think they went?" Corey asked.

"To North Carolina, I think," Grandmother said. "They wanted to open an inn at the beach."

"Not the Cornells," I said. "The ghosts. Where did *they* go?"

Grandmother shrugged. "In my opinion, they were never here in the first place."

"You don't believe in ghosts?" Corey looked surprised.

"Of course not." Grandmother laughed. "But sometimes I find myself wishing they'd come back. Business might improve."

"What do you mean?" I asked.

"You'd be surprised how many people come here because of that stupid book," Grandmother said. "Then they leave in a huff because they didn't see a ghost. Some even want their money back."

"Do you have the book?" I asked.

"Of course." Grandmother got up and led us into the

inn, through the kitchen, and down a hall to a large room in the front of the house. "The library," she said.

Tall windows let in long bars of afternoon light. Several pairs of soft leather armchairs flanked the windows. A matching sofa stood near the door. In front of it was a low table covered with magazines. Books crammed the shelves built into the walls.

Grandmother picked up a thick, well-read paperback and handed it to me. "Page 103," she said.

I sat down on the sofa, and Corey perched beside me. I opened the book to page 103.

The Inn at Fox Hill was built in the late 1700s. Originally a private home, it has changed hands many times. Although I checked old records, the inn's history is sketchy at best. Apparently, it served several purposes— among them, a boardinghouse, a tuberculosis sanitarium, a private school. In 1940, the place was abandoned. For fifteen years, it stood vacant. Weather, neglect, and vandals took their toll. Smothered in ivy and surrounded by weeds, the mansion was soon reduced to a shell of its former self. To passersby, it was the very image of a haunted house.

In 1955, Mr. and Mrs. Stephen Cornell, young vacationers from Boston, saw the building and recognized its potential. They spent more than ten years restoring the house and grounds. In 1967, the Inn at Fox Hill opened for business.

Soon the Cornells began receiving complaints from guests. A woman in a long white dress roamed the grounds at night, moaning so loudly she woke them up.

Others were kept awake by noisy children playing in the halls. Many reported hearing footsteps on the stairs, banging doors, barking dogs, sobs, and laughter. Lights and radios came on in the middle of the night. Water gushed from faucets. Toilets flushed continually. The power went off for no reason—and came back on again for no reason.

Rather amusingly, one woman was especially indignant about an impudent child who called her "Fatso" but who ran away before she got a good look at him. More seriously, several guests complained of theft—watches, rings, jewelry, and the like disappeared from drawers and bedside tables.

Mr. and Mrs. Cornell were as mystified as their guests. They investigated the plumbing and the wiring; they kept doors locked at night; they even hired a night watchman. Nothing helped. The incidents continued.

Soon psychics descended on Fox Hill, followed by ghost hunters with special cameras and recorders. The experts agreed: Ghosts roamed the halls of the inn.

As we all know, some people are sensitive to the presence of ghosts. Others are not. If you want to test yourself, spend a night or two at the Inn at Fox Hill. I did . . . and I was not disappointed! When I woke, the cheap ring I'd left deliberately on the bedside table was gone.

And remember, even if you don't see a ghost, you'll enjoy the Cornells' hospitality, the inn's charm, the fresh Vermont air, the gorgeous scenery, and the meals prepared by the cook in residence, the excellent Mrs. Martha Brewster, a rare marvel.

I closed the book and stared at Grandmother. "Are you sure," I began, but she cut me off with a wave of her hand.

"It's absolute nonsense." She shook her head disdainfully and returned the book to the shelf. "Five thirty," she said. "Time for dinner."

As Corey and I followed Grandmother out of the library, we glanced at each other. Without saying a word, I knew my sister was thinking exactly what I was thinking. Rappings and tappings, footsteps, doors opening and shutting—*we* could do that. And more. Bringing ghosts back to Fox Hill would be like playing haunted house all summer long.

2

The dining room was large enough for at least two dozen people, but only two other tables were occupied. The bike riders sat together by the French doors, open to a view of the mountains. Lean, sunburned guys with huge leg muscles, they didn't look as if they'd come to Vermont to see ghosts.

At another table were Mr. and Mrs. Jennings, who'd showed up just before dinner, wanting a room. They were old but not old old—probably forty or fifty. His hair was gray, and hers was an odd shade of tan (dyed, according to Corey). He wore hiking shorts, a navy T-shirt, and walking sandals over rag-wool socks. "He doesn't want people to see his ugly toes," Corey whispered.

Mrs. Jennings wore shorts and a flowered T-shirt and sandals without socks, showing her perfect red lacquered nails.

All in all, they looked pretty fit for their age, but I doubted they'd come to Vermont to bike or hike. Corey guessed they were antique collectors in search of rusty farm tools to put in their flower garden.

Then we noticed they were reading *Haunted Inns of Vermont*. Grandmother pointedly ignored their taste in literature, but Corey kicked me under the table to make sure I'd noticed.

As promised, the grim and silent Mrs. Brewster produced a great meal: spicy chicken served on rice with some vegetables I shoved aside, a basket of freshly baked rolls, and a salad.

A blonde with a freckled nose served us. She looked about sixteen, I thought. Probably in high school. She was really cute, just the kind of girlfriend I hoped to have someday.

"Tracy," Grandmother said, "these are my grandchildren, Travis and Corey. They'll be here all summer." Smiling at us, she added, "I don't know what I'd do without Tracy. She serves meals, washes dishes, and keeps the inn clean and tidy."

"You'll love it here." Tracy leaned a little closer to Corey and me. "The inn's supposed to be haunted, but so far I haven't seen a thing. Kind of disappointing, actually. I was hoping to have some scary stories to tell when I go back to school."

Grandmother shook her head. "I thought you had better sense."

"I know *you* don't believe in ghosts, Mrs. Donovan," Tracy said. "But you can't prove they don't exist."

"You can't prove they *do* exist, either," Grandmother pointed out.

"Well, why not give them the benefit of the doubt?" Corey asked. "It makes things more interesting."

"That's enough silly talk." Grandmother frowned at Corey's plate. "Eat your dinner before it gets cold."

Tracy left to refill the bike riders' water glasses, and I dug into my dinner, washing it down with gallons of iced tea and topping it off with peach cobbler à la mode. Except for the vegetables, it might have been the best meal I'd ever eaten.

Corey ate most of hers, which was amazing. Usually she picks at her food, which drives Mom and Dad insane. If she doesn't eat enough, they worry she's anorexic. If she eats too much, they worry she's bulimic. I think she just likes the attention.

After dinner, Grandmother dropped into a rocking chair on the porch and gazed at the mountains. The trees cast long shadows toward the inn. High in the sky, swallows dipped and soared, catching bugs on the fly.

The bike riders sat down nearby and spread out their maps to plan the next day's ride. "I say we go this way."

"After today," the other said, "I was hoping to take it easy tomorrow. How about this road along the river?"

"We came up here to get in shape, Tim."

As they argued about their route, the screen door opened and Mrs. Jennings stepped out, *Haunted Inns of Vermont* in her hand.

"Excuse me, Mrs. Donovan," she said, "but my husband and I read about Fox Hill in this book, and we were just wondering—"

Grandmother smiled and shook her head. "I'm sorry to disappoint you, but no one has seen a ghost here for at least three years. Maybe they took their little ectoplasmic selves down to North Carolina with the former owners."

Mrs. Jennings sighed. "According to the author, you have to be in tune with the spirit world to see ghosts. Just because no one has seen them doesn't mean they're not here."

"I'm glad *I* don't have such an ability," Grandmother said pleasantly. "The real world's scary enough for me."

Mr. Jennings joined us just in time to hear the end of

the conversation. "How about you kids?" he asked. "Do you believe in ghosts?"

Corey and I put on serious faces. "Definitely," I said.

"I've *seen* a ghost," Corey added.

"Really?" Mrs. Jennings drew in her breath, obviously ready to believe anything. "What was it like? Can you tell us about it?"

I hid a grin behind my hand. Could she tell them about it? The Jennings didn't know how much my sister loved an audience.

"Well," Corey began, "last winter, I was sleeping over at my friend Julie's house, and something woke me up in the middle of the night. This old lady was standing at the foot of the bed and staring at Julie."

Corey paused a moment to let the suspense grow, I guessed.

"When the old lady realized I was awake," she went on, "she smiled at me and put a finger to her lips. Then, real slowly, she backed away from the bed and walked out of the room, watching Julie all the while, like she was never going to see her again."

The Jenningses hung on every word. Grandmother listened, too—but in her case, she seemed to be wondering what my sister was up to.

"The next morning," Corey said, playing to the Jenningses, "I expected to see Julie's grandmother, but when I asked where she was, Julie's mother said she lived in Pennsylvania. 'Then who was that old lady in Julie's bedroom?' I asked. They all looked at me like I was crazy—even Julie. 'There's no old lady here,' her father said. 'You must have been dreaming.'"

Corey paused to swat a mosquito. "Just then the phone rang," she said, "and Julie's mother went to answer it. First she said, 'No, oh, no.' Then she asked when. And then she started crying."

She took a deep breath and dropped her voice to a whisper. We all leaned closer to hear her. "It turned out Julie's grandmother had died just about the time I saw the old lady. She'd come to say goodbye."

Mrs. Jennings grabbed her husband's hand. "Oh, I'm all over goosebumps."

"Me, too." Corey rubbed her arms as if she were cold. "I can still see that old lady smiling down at Julie."

"Incidents like that are often reported," Mr. Jennings put in. "It's a well-documented phenomenon—the last farewell."

Mrs. Jennings turned to Grandmother. "What do you think now? Surely you believe your own granddaughter."

Grandmother was staring at Corey. "I must admit I didn't know she was such a good storyteller."

Corey wasn't a *good* storyteller—she was a *brilliant* storyteller. No matter what Grandmother thought of Julie's grandmother's last farewell, the Jenningses totally believed Corey. In fact, I almost believed her myself.

While Grandmother rocked silently, the Jenningses told a few ghost stories they'd either read or heard about—last farewells, phantom limousines on deserted roads, old-fashioned ladies in brown who appeared and disappeared in dark hallways.

The bike riders stopped arguing and listened. Tim even threw in a story of mysterious blue lights that hovered over a mountain down south somewhere. His buddy,

Robert, said he didn't believe in that stuff—which earned him a nod of approval from Grandmother.

Tracy joined us and claimed her grandfather had seen his dog's ghost at the very spot on the road where he'd been killed by a car. And her sister once visited a friend's house and saw a lady in a long gray dress walk through a wall and vanish. "The house was really old," she added. "And the people who lived there had seen the ghost themselves."

Gradually, the stories faded away and we sat together silently, each of us thinking our own thoughts—about ghosts, I guessed. Some believing, some not, and some not sure. The moon was almost full, and stars studded the sky—thousands, maybe millions, more than I'd ever seen in New York.

"It's getting chilly." Mrs. Jennings got to her feet with a shiver and headed for the door with Mr. Jennings behind her.

The bike riders yawned and followed the Jenningses. "Big day ahead," Robert said. "At least seventy-five miles."

Tim groaned.

As Tracy started to leave, Grandmother asked her to tell Mr. Brewster she needed him.

A few moments later, a short, bearded man crossed the lawn toward us. For a moment, I thought an ancient garden gnome had come to life, but it turned out to be Mr. Brewster. He wore a frown as permanent as Mrs. Brewster's, made even sterner by his drooping mustache.

"These are my grandchildren, Corey and Travis," Grandmother told him. "They'll be sleeping in the two rooms on the first floor in the back. Can you help them with their luggage?"

Mr. Brewster got our suitcases from the truck and carried them inside as if they were packed with feathers instead of books and shoes and clothes that weighed a ton. Like Mrs. Brewster, he didn't say a word to anyone, just sort of grunted an acknowledgment of Grandmother's request.

"Henry's a bit taciturn," Grandmother said. "But he totes luggage up and down the steps, fixes everything that breaks, and keeps the grounds in shape. In some ways, the two of them run the place."

She laughed as if the Brewsters were lovable characters in a sitcom, but I thought it would be annoying to depend on such cranky people.

We followed her and Mr. Brewster through the kitchen and into an annex built onto the back of the inn.

"This used to be the servants' quarters," Grandmother said, "but the Cornells made it into a modern apartment for themselves."

At the end of a hallway, Mr. Brewster set our luggage down and walked away without a word.

Grandmother opened the doors to two small identical rooms. "I meant to paint the walls and hang new curtains, but somehow I never got around to it. The season started with a dozen bicyclers and then a busload of senior citizens, which was good for business but took all my time."

"It's great," I said. "A bed, a bureau, a table, a chair, and a lamp. What more do I need?"

Corey nodded. "You should see the cabin I had at

camp last summer—four bunk beds, eight girls, and an outhouse a mile away."

Grandmother smiled and excused herself. "It's been a long day. If you two don't mind, I'll go to bed and leave you to unpack."

As soon as she left, I followed Corey into her room, almost identical to mine. "Where did you come up with that granny story?"

"I saw it on a TV show about ghosts. The Jenningses really ate it up, didn't they?"

"Are you thinking what I'm thinking?"

Corey grinned. "Ghosts are about to reappear at the inn," she said. "In fact, I predict the Jenningses will have their own experience with the supernatural before they leave."

"They'll go home and tell other people," I said, "who'll come to the inn hoping to see ghosts. They won't be disappointed."

"Soon Fox Hill will be booked up every night," Corey went on. "Grandmother will have to turn people away."

"They'll camp out in the yard."

"They'll look in the windows."

"There'll be a traffic jam from here to Burlington."

"The Learning Channel will send a team of psychics and ghost hunters."

"We'll be on the evening news."

"Anderson Cooper will do a week long special on CNN."

"Someone will write a book like *The Amityville Horror*."

"It'll be a bestseller."

"They'll make a movie of it!"

"We'll star in it!"

"We'll be famous!"

By this time, we were shouting and laughing and jumping on Corey's bed.

"Travis!" Grandmother shouted from the doorway. "Corey! What on earth is all this ruckus?"

We tried to stop laughing. "We're just fooling around," I said while Corey hiccupped hysterically.

"Well, please calm down," Grandmother said. "You'll disturb the guests."

That made Corey and me laugh again. Grandmother had no idea how disturbed the guests were going to be.

"It's almost ten, and you haven't even started unpacking," she said with a frown. "At the risk of sounding like a camp counselor, I suggest you save that task for tomorrow, put on your pajamas, and go to bed."

"We're sorry," I said, making a real effort to sound sincere, but I hadn't quite gotten the laughter out of my voice.

"Don't be mad," Corey added, faking much better than I had. "We're just so excited to be here. I guess we got carried away."

Grandmother came into the room and gave us each a kiss. "I'm not mad. Just tired. Now settle down and go to sleep."

After she left, I went to my room and put on my pajamas. When I tapped on Corey's door, she said, "Come in."

Still wearing her shorts and T-shirt, she was rummaging through her suitcase, scattering clothes everywhere. At last she found what she was looking for.

She held up a white nightgown and swirled it in front of me. "At breakfast, I'll tell the Jenningses I saw a ghost in a long white dress, flitting around under the trees—like the ghost in the haunted inns book."

"How do you know they'll believe you?"

"They believed the granny story, didn't they?" Corey smoothed the gown. "People like the Jenningses are easy to fool because they *want* to see ghosts. You don't have to convince them—they already believe. All I have to do is go outside tomorrow night wearing this and they'll think they're seeing a real ghost."

"But won't they recognize you?"

Corey sighed the way she always did when she thought I was too stupid to be her brother.

"We'll ride bikes to Middlebury and buy white make-up and that black stuff teenagers use on their eyes. Maybe we can find a long filmy scarf to hide my hair. After Grandmother goes to bed tomorrow night, I'll smear my face dead white and make big dark circles under my eyes, like empty eye sockets. I'll put on my nightgown and dance around under the trees in a scary way, moaning and groaning. Maybe I'll even shriek." She frowned. "Too bad I didn't bring my Vampira costume from last Halloween. It would've been perfect, but who knew I'd need it up here?"

"So that's the plan—you impersonate a ghost and scare the Jenningses, and they go home and spread the word?"

Corey grinned. "It's a start. We can think of more stuff, like footsteps and moans and groans and crying babies."

"And howling dogs and rappings and tappings and strange blue lights."

By the time I went back to my own room and climbed into bed, I was too excited to sleep. I lay awake a long time, my mind racing with ideas. With Corey's and my help, Grandmother would be a rich woman by the end of the summer.

3

The next morning, Corey and I found the Jenningses on the patio, drinking coffee. I leaned against the trellis, slightly embarrassed, but Corey sat down between them. Without hesitating, she whispered, "Did you see it last night?"

"See what, dear?" Mrs. Jennings nibbled at her croissant, her eyes fixed on my sister.

Corey drew a deep breath and somehow managed to look pale. "The ghost."

"Ghost?" Croissant in midair, Mrs. Jennings gasped. "You saw a *ghost* last night?"

"Shh," Corey hissed. "Grandmother told me not to tell anyone. She insists I imagined it, but I swear I saw it."

"After that story you told, I knew you were sensitive to the spirit world." Mr. Jennings looked at Corey with awe.

"Tell us everything. Don't leave out a single detail." Mrs. Jennings kept her voice so low I had to move closer to hear her.

"Something woke me around three A.M.," Corey said. "That's the demons' hour, you know—halfway between midnight and dawn."

"Yes, yes." Mrs. Jennings patted Corey's hand. "Go on."

"Well, I went to my window," Corey said. "At first, I didn't see anything, but I heard sort of a low moaning sound." As she spoke, a gust of wind skittered across the table, blowing the paper napkins onto the lawn. Mrs. Jennings shivered.

"Then I saw this woman in white," Corey went on, "flitting about under the trees. For a moment, she looked toward the house, straight at me, and I ducked behind the curtain. When I got the nerve to look again, she was gone."

Mrs. Jennings leaned toward Corey. "What did she look like?"

"She was wearing a long white dress, and her face was really hideous—white as a skull with dark circles where her eyes should be." Corey shuddered. "She moaned and groaned and then shrieked, like a banshee or something."

"I heard it, too!" Mrs. Jennings whispered. "But I didn't know what it was."

"You must have been terrified," Mr. Jennings said.

"I'm still shaking." Corey held out her trembling hands as proof. "It was definitely evil. Not sweet like Julie's grandmother. Wicked."

"Oh, my goodness." Mrs. Jennings stared at my sister. "Oh, my dear, how absolutely dreadful."

The breeze danced in the flower bed, shaking the blossoms. Wind chimes clinked like someone laughing. For a moment, I thought I saw something move in the shifting shadows under the trees.

Mr. Jennings turned to me. "Did you see it, too, Travis?"

This was my sister's show, so I shook my head. "Corey ran into my room and woke me up. I've never seen her so scared. In fact, she scared *me*. She's really psychic, you know." Psycho was more like it, but why spoil things with the truth?

"Do you think the ghost walks . . . every night?" Mr. Jennings asked, voice low, practically quivering with excitement.

"Ghosts usually do the same thing over and over again," Corey said. "Like they're atoning for something they did—or didn't do—while they were alive."

Mrs. Jennings sighed with envy. "Sometimes I get feelings, sensations, a sort of shiver. But I've never actually seen anything."

"Nor have I," Mr. Jennings admitted sadly. "We've gone to many so-called haunted inns, but we've been disappointed every time."

To keep from laughing, Corey avoided looking at me. "Get up at three A.M. tomorrow and watch those trees." She pointed at a grove of oaks. Even in the morning sun, the shadows they cast seemed denser and darker than anywhere else. "*That's* where I saw the ghost," she said.

The Jenningses stared at the grove as if they hoped to catch a glimpse of the ghost in broad daylight. "We'll be watching," Mrs. Jennings promised.

Mr. Jennings set his coffee mug down with a clink and got to his feet. "In the meantime, Louise and I have sightseeing plans."

"And some shopping to do," Mrs. Jennings put in. "I want to visit the glass factory near Quechee and browse in a few antique shops on the way. There's a cheese store, too, and an artist's studio. . . ."

We watched them get into their car and drive away. Corey grinned at me. "They won't be disappointed tonight."

A couple of hours later, we parked our bikes in front of a tourist-bait shop on Middlebury's main drag and went inside. We found white and green face makeup, black stuff for Corey's eyes, dark purple lipstick, and a bunch of other junk—rubber eyeballs that glowed in the dark, plastic spiders and rubber snakes, spray-on cobwebs, a haunted-house sound-effects CD, a lantern, candles, and flashlights that cast a blue beam. In a secondhand store, Corey bought a long white filmy scarf.

By the time we'd eaten a couple of slices of pizza and washed them down with bottles of soda, we'd spent about a quarter of our entire summer's allowance. And we had a fifteen-mile ride back to Fox Hill, mostly uphill this time. Balancing our shopping bags on the handlebars, we set off for the inn.

We spent the rest of the afternoon at the pool. We'd swim for a while, then lie in the sun and plan our ghost act, then dive back into the water. We had the place to ourselves. The bike riders had pedaled off to add more muscle to their legs, the Jenningses were still touring the countryside, and Grandmother was sitting on the patio dozing over a novel. Every now and then, Mr. Brewster cruised past on a riding mower, pretty much ruining the peace and quiet. He never looked our way.

At dinner, a new guest joined us. Mr. Nelson was short and skinny. He reminded me of a really strict math teacher who gave me a C and ruined my report card in sixth grade. He sat at a table by himself, reading a science book propped open with his saltshaker—*Global Warming in Our Lifetime: Fact or Myth?* It was clear he had no wish to be sociable. Why make friends when the world is about to end?

The Jenningses talked Tracy's ear off with tales of their day of shopping, the lovely lunch they'd eaten, the bargains they'd found. Cheese! Barn-board paintings! Pure Vermont maple syrup! A rusty child's wagon for the garden back home!

While they chattered, the bike riders discussed their ride—seventy-five miles in five hours, a near miss with a logging truck, an eagle sighting, a flat tire. Tim was making a major effort to stay awake, but Robert looked ready to hop on his bike and ride another fifty miles before bedtime.

After we'd eaten, everyone congregated on the porch again. Mr. Nelson sat at the end of the row of rocking chairs and kept his nose in his book. While Tim dozed, Robert studied his map, obviously planning another grueling ride. The Jenningses darted little looks at Corey and me, probably eager to talk to us alone.

When it was too dark to see the map, Robert woke Tim up. Mr. Nelson closed his book. They said good night and went to their rooms. A few minutes later, Grandmother excused herself.

As soon as she left, the Jenningses parked themselves in rockers next to ours.

"What a perfect night for a sighting." Mr. Jennings pointed to the full moon rising above the mountains.

"Bright light, no clouds. If the ghost comes, we'll get a good look at it."

"I'm not sure I want to see her again," Corey said. "She was pretty scary."

"I plan to sleep like a log," I put in. "No ghosts for me."

"Not us," Mr. Jennings said. "We'll be wide awake."

A cool breeze swept across the porch, rocking the empty chairs as it passed. The shadows of the morning glory draping the porch trellis quivered and shifted, and the wind chimes laughed on the dark lawn.

Mrs. Jennings pulled her sweater tighter and stood up. "It's getting cold."

"We're in Vermont," Mr. Jennings said.

Giving his wife a little hug, he said good night to us, and the two of them went up to bed.

By two thirty A.M., Corey had caked her face with white makeup, hollowed out her cheeks with green eye shadow, circled her eyes with black, and coated her mouth with purple lipstick. The scarf hid her hair.

"Do I look horrible enough?" she asked.

"If you looked any worse, *I'd* be scared of you."

We sneaked out the back door and ran across the lawn. Taking care not to be seen, we darted into the inky blackness of the oak grove. Anchored to earth with its shadow, the inn was dark. Everyone was asleep—except the Jenningses. Although we couldn't see them, we knew they were peering out their window, waiting to see the ghost.

Corey stepped onto the moonlit grass. Waving her arms slowly and dramatically, she glided along, sleeves and scarf fluttering. She dipped and swayed, she moaned and groaned, and then turned to stare at the inn. Stretching both arms, she pointed her fingers, threw back her head, and screamed.

Over my head, the leaves on the trees rustled and shook, as if Corey had awakened sleeping squirrels and birds. Something twittered softly, and the bushes swayed.

With goosebumps racing across my skin, I watched Corey run toward me. "Quick!" she hissed. "We have to get back to bed before anyone comes looking for us."

As she spoke, lights went on in the inn and the carriage house, and someone shouted.

Fearing we'd be caught, I ran after Corey. At the back door, she dragged me inside and we dashed to our rooms. I jumped into bed and burrowed under the covers.

Moments later, Grandmother called, "Travis? Are you awake?"

I pushed back the blanket and sat up, blinking at her. "Wha'?" I croaked, trying to sound as if she'd waked me from deep sleep. "Hunh?"

"I heard a noise." She went to my window and peered out. "It sounded like it came from that grove of trees."

"Didn't hear it," I muttered and lay back down.

Grandmother went to my sister's door. "Corey?"

"Asleep," she murmured. "Didn't hear."

"It must have been a screech owl." Grandmother sounded as if she was trying to convince herself. "I'm sorry I woke you." The door closed, and the inn was silent again.

I curled up under the covers and tried not to laugh out loud. We'd done it—ghosts had returned to Fox Hill.

After a while, I heard Corey tiptoeing down the hall to the bathroom. She was in there a long time, but before she went back to her room, she stopped to see me.

"Boy, was that stuff hard to get off. My whole face stings." She touched her cheek and winced. "If I hadn't found some cold cream, I'd still be scrubbing."

"You were great," I told her.

She bounced on the bed and laughed. "I think I woke up *everybody* with that scream."

"People for miles around heard you," I told her. "The cows won't give milk tomorrow, the chickens won't lay eggs, and the corn will wither on the stalks."

"Black dogs will turn white overnight." Corey laughed. "Flowers will drop their petals."

"Barns will collapse," I shouted. "Chimneys will topple!"

"Shh," Corey hushed me. "You'll wake Grandmother."

I clapped my hand over my mouth and tried to stop laughing.

Corey hugged herself in delight. "I can't wait to hear what everybody says tomorrow!"

4

The next morning, Corey and I found the Jenningses waiting for us in the dining room.

"We saw it!" Mr. Jennings whispered. "We actually saw it. And *heard* it."

"It pointed at us and screamed." Mrs. Jennings pressed a hand against her heart. "It was terrifying."

Corey feigned disappointment. "Oh, no, I must have slept right through it." She glanced at me. "Did you see it?"

I shook my head, trying to look as bummed as Corey. "I guess I was really tired."

By then, the bike riders had joined us. "Are you talking about that noise last night?" Tim asked.

"What was it?" Robert wanted to know. "A cougar or something?"

Mrs. Jennings stared at him. "You didn't see it?"

Robert shook his head. "It woke us up, but by the time we got to the window, it was gone."

"If it was a cougar, we should stay off the trails," Tim said. "A few years ago, one of those big cats killed a bike rider in California."

At that moment, Mr. Brewster walked past on his way to the kitchen. "That was no cougar," he muttered.

"Are you sure?" Robert asked.

"Of course I'm sure." Mr. Brewster stopped and

scowled as if Robert had called him a liar. "I've lived in Vermont all my life, so I ought to know what a cougar sounds like."

It was the most I'd ever heard him say.

"If it wasn't a cougar, what was it?" Tim asked, his eyes widening like a kid's at a horror movie.

Mr. Brewster had already lost interest in the subject. With a shake of his head, he disappeared into the kitchen, leaving us to stare after him.

"A ghost," Mrs. Jennings said. "It was a ghost."

Robert laughed. "That's ridiculous."

Mrs. Jennings frowned at Robert. "My husband and I saw it ourselves—as plain as plain can be, by that grove of trees." Mrs. Jennings waved her hand toward the window and the oaks. "It pointed at the inn and screamed in the most hideous, inhuman way!"

Robert laughed again, but Tim just stood there, as if he wasn't sure what to think.

Mr. Jennings laid a hand on my sister's shoulder. "This young lady saw it the night before last."

Corey shuddered. "It was awful."

Before Robert could say anything sarcastic, Tim grabbed his arm. "Lay off, will you? *You* didn't see it. *They* did."

Across the room, Mr. Nelson looked up from his newspaper. "So the ghosts are back," he said. "I was hoping they'd gone for good."

Just then, Grandmother came into the dining room. Tracy was right behind her, carrying a tray heaped with breakfast goodies. "What's back?" Grandmother asked.

"The ghosts." Mr. Nelson grimaced. "Didn't you hear the screams last night?"

Tracy gasped and almost dropped the tray. "I thought it was a screech owl."

"I heard what *sounded* like a scream," Grandmother said. "I must admit it scared me, but after I went back to bed, I realized what it was."

Corey and I darted a quick glance at each other. Had Grandmother guessed we'd played a prank on the Jenningses? I held my breath and waited for her to denounce us.

"Some people a mile or so down the road breed peacocks," she went on. "One must have flown the coop—so to speak." She smiled at her own joke. "A peacock's cry sounds remarkably like a human scream."

"There," Robert said to Tim. "I *knew* there was a rational explanation."

"But what about the ghost?" Tim asked. "All three of them have seen it."

Grandmother looked at us, plainly annoyed. "You were talking about ghosts the other night, swapping stories, trying to scare each other," she said. "You expected to see a ghost, and you've convinced yourselves you did."

Mrs. Jennings frowned at Grandmother. "I didn't *imagine* that ghost. If you'd been at your window, you would've seen it, too."

"You were looking out the window at three A.M.?" Robert asked in disbelief.

"Corey saw the ghost the night before at exactly three A.M.," Mrs. Jennings said. "She told George and me to watch for it in the grove of trees."

I held my breath, hoping the phone or the doorbell

would ring—anything to distract Grandmother from questioning my sister and me.

Unfortunately, no one called and no one came to the door. Grandmother fixed Corey with a steely gaze. "You never mentioned seeing a ghost."

Unable to meet Grandmother's eyes, Corey stared at the floor. "You wouldn't have believed me," she whispered. "But I saw it and I was scared and I told Mrs. Jennings because I knew *she'd* believe me."

While we were talking, Mr. Nelson had gone back to reading his newspaper.

I sidled over to him. "Why did you say the ghosts were back? Have you seen them before?"

He put down the paper with some irritation. "I've been coming to Fox Hill every July for twenty years," he said. "I remember the purported ghosts, as well as the reporters and the psychics and the nuts who came to witness the goings-on. They swarmed upstairs and down, ranting about cold spots, setting up bizarre recording devices and infrared cameras, making nuisances of themselves. Fools, that's what they were. Idiots." He took a sip of coffee. "The inn is much better off without ghosts," he said, "and the maniacs who flocked here to see them—*they* caused the most disturbance, by far."

Across the room, Robert seated himself noisily. "Get a move on, Tim," he said in a loud you-can't-fool-me voice. "We're doing a century ride today."

Before he joined his friend, Tim smiled at Corey. "My girlfriend is psychic, too," he told her. "She sees all kinds of things, just like you do—including those blue lights I was telling you about the other night."

Grandmother watched Tim join Robert at their table. Turning to Corey, she said, "I don't know what you're up to, but I simply do not believe one word of this ghost nonsense."

To the rest of us, she said, "Breakfast is ready. Please take your seats, and Tracy will serve you."

Corey and I sat down, and Grandmother sat between us. "No more ghost talk," she said. "I won't have you scaring the guests with silly stories."

Corey kicked me under the table, and I kicked her back. She giggled.

"I'm serious," Grandmother said.

We both nodded and turned our attention to the plates Tracy set down in front of us—scrambled eggs with cheese, home-fried potatoes, and a big cranberry muffin.

That afternoon, three couples, all friends of the Jenningses, arrived and requested rooms. Mrs. Jennings had told them about the ghost sighting and they were full of questions. Grandmother became increasingly annoyed, but no matter what she said, the new guests refused to be discouraged. If the Jenningses had seen a ghost, the ghost was real. And they wanted to see it themselves.

"Aren't you glad you have more guests?" Corey asked at dinnertime.

"Not if they're coming to see ghosts," Grandmother said. "They're bound to be disappointed." Sipping her iced tea, her expression as sour as a lemon, she regarded the four couples huddled around a table by the window.

Mrs. Jennings was describing the screaming phantom

to her friends. "It pointed right at me, and cursed me. Not George. Me. It cursed *me*."

"Oh, my goodness," Mrs. Bennett, one of the new guests, gasped. "You must have been terrified."

As Mrs. Jennings shivered, Mr. Jennings said, "You should have seen its eyes. They were red, and they glowed like hellfire."

"Oh, for heaven's sake," Grandmother muttered more to herself than to Corey and me. "This is getting more ridiculous by the moment."

Without waiting for Tracy to bring coffee, she left the dining room. The others followed her outside, chatting noisily. Corey went to the library to read, and I followed Tracy into the kitchen.

"Do you think Mrs. Jennings really saw a ghost?" I asked.

She looked up from a sinkful of soapy dishes. "Maybe," she said slowly. "But I can't be sure unless I see it myself."

"Wouldn't you be scared?" I was hoping she'd say yes and faint in my arms or something, but she merely shrugged. Without even looking at me, she said, "Ghosts can't hurt you."

Mrs. Brewster laid a heavy hand on my shoulder. "Unless you want to help Tracy clean up," she said, "I suggest you find someone else to talk to."

Taking the hint, I left Tracy to her dishes and went outside. Grandmother was sitting in a lawn chair, enjoying the last of the sunset, Robert and Tim were playing a relaxed game of tennis, and Mr. Nelson had settled himself in a rocking chair, his face hidden behind the evening paper. The Jennings party was seated in a circle, taking turns reading from the haunted inns book.

No one noticed me stroll across the lawn to the haunted grove—as Mr. and Mrs. Jennings now called it. The sun had just sunk behind the mountains, and the air was growing cool and damp. A breeze rustled the leaves, and a bird called. As I stood in the shadows, looking at the inn, I had a sudden feeling I wasn't alone.

Expecting to see my sister, I glanced behind me. No one was there, but the feeling lingered. "Corey?"

I peered into the shadows gathering under the trees. For a second, I thought I saw something duck out of sight behind one of the tall oaks.

"Hey," I called. "I see you." My voice sounded loud in the quiet evening—and a little high pitched, almost as though I was scared. Which, of course, I wasn't.

No one answered. Leaves rustled, and something on the ground snapped—maybe a branch cracking under a foot, maybe an animal scurrying past unseen.

With a shiver, I left the grove and hurried back to the inn. I told myself I'd heard a squirrel or a bird. But I couldn't shake the feeling that someone had been watching me.

5

In the middle of a bad dream, I woke up to see a hideous face hanging over me in the dark.

"Wake up, Travis," it moaned. "It's time to go to the grove."

"No, no!" I pushed the thing away from me, only to hear it laugh.

"Fooled you," Corey crowed.

"Brat," I muttered, too embarrassed to come up with a clever retort.

"It's time for the ghost to walk." Corey glided toward the door.

Shoving my blankets aside, I got out of bed and tiptoed outside behind my fearless sister. As soon as I stepped into the shadows under the trees, I began to shiver, just as I had earlier. The night seemed darker here, colder, spookier. The leaves whispered, the shadows shifted and changed and formed new shapes.

I glanced at Corey, but she didn't appear to notice anything out of the ordinary. With a giggle, she danced across the grass, waving her arms dramatically, her head thrown back, her filmy nightgown fluttering. Just as she had the previous night, she stopped suddenly, turned toward the inn, and screamed loudly. The echo made it sound as if a dozen ghosts—or a hundred peacocks—were shrieking an answer.

With one more piercing scream, Corey fled into the

shadows, and the two of us raced back to the inn. Again, I sensed someone close by, not just watching me this time but following me. Someone silent and swift, darker even than the night. I wanted to look back, just to prove nothing was there, but I didn't dare.

Corey usually outran me, but a surge of adrenaline sent me speeding into the inn well ahead of her.

I dove into bed just before Grandmother poked her head into my room. "Travis?" she whispered, "are you awake?"

I lay still, eyes tightly closed, breathing deep, regular breaths.

She closed my door, and I heard her go to my sister's room. "Corey?"

No answer. I pictured Corey huddled under the covers, made up to look like a ghost from your worst nightmare, and hoped Grandmother wouldn't pull the blankets back.

Soon I heard Grandmother return to her bedroom— where she probably lay awake pondering the noisy peacocks down the road.

I snuggled deeper into bed. Between talking about the hauntings and playing the ghost game, I'd set myself up to imagine I'd been watched in the grove and followed to the inn. As Grandmother said about the Jenningses, I was obviously susceptible. Nothing was in the grove. Nothing had followed me. It was ridiculous. *I* was ridiculous.

But what was that noise in the hall? Was someone standing just outside my room, ear pressed to my door? I lay still and listened so hard my ears buzzed. Nothing. . . . No, *not* nothing. A tiny creak, a flutter in the air, a cold draft across my face, a whisper of sound almost like a giggle.

"Corey, is that you?" I sat up and peered into the darkness. I was alone in my room.

Feeling foolish, I lay back down and pulled the blanket over my head. The loudest sound was my heart pounding. I might as well have been five years old.

In the morning, the guests gathered in the dining room to talk about the screaming ghost. The newcomers were almost too excited to eat the waffles Mrs. Brewster had prepared.

After Grandmother left the room to take a phone call, Tracy came to our table. "I heard the scream last night." She smoothed her hair back behind her ears and grinned. "Tonight, I'm going to camp out in the grove—I want to see the ghost for myself. You know, up close and personal."

Corey and I glanced at each other, frozen for a second. "You'd better not," I said. "No matter what you think, that ghost is definitely dangerous."

"Don't be silly." Tracy laughed.

Mrs. Brewster stuck her head out of the kitchen and gestured to the bicyclists' table. Tracy turned and noticed Robert holding up his coffee cup. "Excuse me," she murmured to Corey and me. "I'd better get back to work before the old battle-ax fires me."

As Tracy fetched coffee for Robert, Corey and I left the inn and settled into a pair of Adirondack chairs at the shady end of the lawn. "Do you think she'll go to the grove tonight?" Corey asked.

"If she does, she won't see anything."

"What do you mean?" Corey frowned as if she suspected I was about to edge her out of the starring role in our little drama.

"We'll be inside," I said, "trying some new tricks. Footsteps. Doors opening and shutting. Sobs and moans and spooky laughter."

We got up and ambled across the lawn, talking about things we could do with flashlights and string and sound effects. Without noticing where we were going, we ended up in the grove. Even in the daylight, it was a gloomy place. The shade seemed too dark, the air too cold, too still. Moss grew thick on the damp ground and furred the tree trunks. Toadstools sprouted everywhere, some red, some yellow, some white—all poisonous, I was sure. A crow watched us mournfully from a high branch, but no birds sang.

Corey shivered and folded her arms across her chest. "Tracy's a lot braver than I am. I wouldn't sleep here by myself. Not if you paid me."

"Me, either." I glanced at her. "Last night I swear somebody was hiding here in the shadows, watching us."

Corey drew in her breath and hugged herself tighter. "I thought it was my imagination."

We were both whispering, as if someone might be listening as well as watching. When the crow cawed from its perch overhead, we both jumped and then tried to pass it off with a laugh.

"Let's go," Corey said. "This place gives me the creeps."

We left the grove and wandered through a sunny patch of weedy ground, leaping with grasshoppers and humming with bees. Wild thistles grew taller than our heads.

A narrow path led toward a dilapidated shed and the remains of a barn, its roof fallen in and its walls collapsed. Vines and brambles crawled and curled over the weathered wood, prying the boards apart.

Corey stopped suddenly and pointed at a row of small square stones barely visible among the weeds. "What are those?"

We knelt down to look closer. A two-digit number had been chiseled into each stone, but years of rain and snow made them almost illegible.

"They must mean something," I said.

"But what?"

I shook my head, puzzled.

Losing interest, Corey pushed her hair back from her face. "It's boiling hot. Let's go swimming."

She headed toward the inn, but instead of following her, I stood there, contemplating the row of stones. "Forty-one," I read, "forty-two, forty-three, forty-four." My eyes moved from stone to stone. There were twelve of them. And many more in other rows, all numbered.

"Travis," Corey yelled. "Are you coming?"

Suddenly aware of the heat and the gnats buzzing around my head, I ran to catch up with my sister.

Corey and I spent the rest of the morning in the pool, then got dressed and went to the dining room for lunch. Robert and Tim had checked out that morning to explore New Hampshire's White Mountains. Mr. Nelson was gone, too, claiming he had no desire to experience any more supernatural manifestations. The Jennings gang was still there, along with a new couple from Albany who'd already been drawn into the ghost conversation.

Just as I took a bite of my hamburger, another new-comer swept into the room. Short and plump, with a head of frizzy blond curls, she wore layers of dark gauzy clothes that seemed to float in the air around her. Her arms clanked with silver and copper bracelets. She sported a ring on each of her chubby fingers, as well as a few on her round little toes, and a small silver hoop in one nostril. Earrings dangled to her shoulders in a shower of stars. Her scarlet lipstick matched her nail polish. She'd taken care to coat her eyelids green and spike her lashes with mascara.

With much twittering, she joined the group at the Jenningses' table.

"Don't stare," Grandmother whispered.

"Who is she?" Rude or not, neither Corey nor I could take our eyes off the woman.

"Miss Eleanor Duvall," Grandmother said with a sniff. "A self-proclaimed ghost hunter."

"Really?"

Grandmother tapped Corey's wrist. "Eat your ham-burger and stop looking at her. I'm sure she loves the attention."

Despite Grandmother's injunction, Corey and I watched Miss Duvall as if she'd hypnotized us.

By the time we'd finished eating, Grandmother was thoroughly annoyed with both of us. "You're from New York," she said. "You must see people like her every day."

We shook our heads. Even in the East Village, Miss Duvall would have stood out from the crowd.

"Oh, no," Grandmother muttered. "She's coming this way."

Indeed she was, followed by the Jenningses and all their friends.

"Don't talk to her about your so-called ghost sightings," Grandmother warned Corey. "Or we'll never get rid of her."

"I'm Edna Frothingham," one of the newcomers said. "And this is Miss Eleanor Duvall, the world-famous psychic and ghost hunter. I called her as soon as I heard from the Jenningses."

Miss Duvall bared a mouthful of tiny teeth in a smile aimed at Corey. "You're the little girl who sees ghosts," she proclaimed, jangling her bracelets like a musical accompaniment.

Just then the phone rang, forcing Grandmother to excuse herself. "Not a word," she hissed in Corey's ear.

But of course Corey couldn't resist a chance to take center stage. "Yes," she said modestly. "I see ghosts all the time."

"Lovely." Miss Duvall sat down in Grandmother's chair. The others gathered around the table, hanging on every word their new leader uttered.

Corey told her about the granny ghost, the ghost of the haunted grove, and the other presences she felt in the inn—the crying baby she heard late at night, the footsteps in the hall outside her door, the sobs, moans, and spooky laughter, the howling dog, and so on. There was no end to her imaginings.

Obviously enjoying herself, my sister had everyone's total attention. Even Tracy drew near, clutching a tray to her chest, her eyes wide, her mouth half open.

"You are truly gifted," Miss Duvall whispered to

Corey. To the others she said, "Often it is children who are most in touch with the spirit world. It is to be expected. After all, they are closer to the other side than we. As the great poet William Wordsworth says, 'Our birth is but a sleep and a forgetting. . . . Heaven lies about us in our infancy.'"

The Jennings gang nodded solemnly, as if they all knew Wordsworth by heart and understood exactly what Miss Duvall meant. Which was more than I could say for myself.

"When I first spoke with Corey, I knew she was special," Mrs. Jennings said, taking the role of my sister's discoverer.

Miss Duvall turned to me. "And how about you, Travis? Do you share your sister's powers?"

Taken by surprise, I said, "Sometimes I sense things. Like the grove. It's, it's—I can't explain it, but—"

"The grove, yes!" Miss Duvall rose from the table in a whirl of gauze and a tinkle of jewelry. "Take me there. I must see it!"

With some reluctance, Corey and I led the whole group of adults across the lawn and into the grove. Immediately, they all began to shiver. The woman from Albany made the sign of the cross, and her husband mumbled a prayer. Mrs. Jennings said she felt faint and took her husband's arm. Her friends gathered closely about Miss Duvall.

"Are you all right, Eleanor?" Mrs. Frothingham asked.

Eyes closed, Miss Duvall swayed as if she'd fallen into a trance. With outstretched arms, she turned in a slow circle, breathing heavily. "Come forth," she whispered. "Show yourself, spirit of darkness. I fear you not."

She stood still and waited. Nothing happened. Nothing that we could see or hear, that is. But something was there. Something that sent shivers racing up and down my spine and prickled my scalp. Corey actually reached for my hand and held it tightly, something she wouldn't do normally.

Opening her eyes at last, Miss Duvall stared at us, the dim light silvering her hair. "It is here," she whispered, "just as the child said. But it does not wish to reveal itself. Perhaps there are too many of us."

With a nervous gesture, she smoothed her clothing and took Corey's other hand. "Come," she said, "we'll return tomorrow when Chester arrives."

"Chester?" I asked.

"Chester Coakley, my associate," Miss Duvall explained. "He was delayed by a nasty piece of business in Salem but should arrive tomorrow with our equipment."

Once we left the grove, the guests began babbling away about the presence in the trees. If Corey and I hadn't felt the thing ourselves, we would've had a good laugh at their expense.

That night, Corey and I made plans for some new tricks. Well after midnight, we tiptoed out of Grandmother's apartment, through the silent kitchen, and into the hall. Scarcely breathing, we crept up the stairs. Moonlight streamed through the tall window on the landing.

"Look. There's Tracy." Corey pointed outside.

We watched the girl cross the lawn, lighting her way with a flashlight. After she vanished into the grove's shadows, we lingered for a moment, watching her light appear and disappear among the trees.

"Just like Nancy Drew," Corey whispered.

"Don't go to the grove, Nancy," I intoned in a spooky voice. "Don't open that door, don't go down those steps, stay out of the attic, watch your—"

"Shut up." Corey hustled me up the stairs.

At the top, we paused and listened. Except for a chorus of snores, all was silent. The guests' doors were closed. No lights showed. At the opposite end of the hall were the back stairs, our escape route to the kitchen.

We looked at each other, and I nodded. Corey began to sob in a high breathless voice, and I waved a tiny pocket flashlight. Its faint blue light barely lit the darkness. Under our bare feet, the floor boards squeaked and creaked. I tapped at one door, then another, and laughed a horrible laugh.

As the guests began shouting and stumbling about in their rooms, we ran silently down the stairs and hid under the kitchen table.

Upstairs, Miss Duvall screeched joyfully, "Sobs, rappings, laughter, footsteps, a blue light—a classic visitation!"

Grandmother opened the door of her apartment and stepped into the kitchen. From our hiding place, Corey and I watched her bare feet pad past.

As soon as she headed upstairs to quiet the guests, my sister and I scurried back to our rooms and jumped into bed. We'd done it again.

I would've laughed out loud if Tracy hadn't screamed somewhere outside in the dark.

By the time Corey and I reached the front door, Grandmother and the guests had gathered around Tracy.

"What's wrong?" Grandmother asked her. "What were

you doing outside at this time of night? I promised your mother I'd make sure you behaved—"

"I went to the grove," Tracy sobbed. "To see the ghost, and it, oh, Mrs. Donovan, it, it—" She collapsed into Grandmother's arms, weeping.

"We heard the ghost, too," Miss Duvall put in, her voice rising. "It was roaming the hall, sobbing and moaning."

"There was a blue light," Mrs. Bennett added.

"Blue," her husband agreed. "But very dim. Spectral."

"It pounded on our door," Mr. Jennings added. "It laughed like a maniac."

"There must be *two* ghosts!" Mrs. Jennings cried. "One outside and one inside."

"Maybe more," Mrs. Frothingham whispered.

Finally, Miss Duvall turned to Tracy, who was still crying in Grandmother's arms. "What did you see?"

"I didn't *see* anything," Tracy sobbed. "But something was there, I *felt* it, it was cold and horrible. Evil." She clung to Grandmother and cried harder.

Corey and I stared at each other. We could explain the inside ghost, but the outside ghost was beginning to frighten both of us.

Keeping one arm around Tracy, Grandmother said, "I think it's time we all went to bed and got some sleep. Tomorrow I'll ask Martha what she put in her tomato sauce—it must have been pretty potent."

If Grandmother had hoped for a laugh, she was disappointed.

"Don't blame the food," Miss Duvall said. "This inn is haunted. Just wait till Chester sets up his equipment tomorrow! Then you'll see."

With that, she flounced upstairs, her gaudy silk robe and nightgown fluttering, her bare feet seemingly too tiny to bear her weight. Even without jewelry and makeup, she was an amazing sight.

The other guests followed her, murmuring to each other about the sobs and laughter, the blue light, and the terrifying presence in the haunted grove.

Flashlight in hand, Grandmother led Tracy back to her room in the carriage house, and Corey and I went to bed. For once we didn't feel like talking about the ghosts of Fox Hill. Or even thinking about them.

6

The next day, Corey and I cornered Tracy in the kitchen. She'd been surrounded by guests all morning, and we wanted to talk to her alone.

"Tell us what happened," Corey begged.

"Every detail," I added. "Don't leave anything out."

Tracy shook her head. "Can't you see I've got dishes to wash?"

Mrs. Brewster looked up from the laundry she'd been sorting. "Go ahead. Tell them. I'd like to hear it myself."

All three of us stared at her, surprised by her interest. Without looking at us, she went on separating white napkins from blue napkins.

"I don't want to talk about it anymore," Tracy murmured.

"You've told everybody else, but I haven't heard a word." Mrs. Brewster frowned at a red sock. "How did that get in with the table linens?"

"Okay," Tracy said, gulping a little. "I wanted to see the ghost—which was totally stupid—so I went to the grove and waited for it to come. After a while, I started hearing a lot of rustling sounds, like squirrels or mice in the leaves." Without looking at us, she paused to wipe her soapy hands on her apron. "Then I thought I saw a face."

"Are you sure it wasn't one of these two playing tricks on you?" Mrs. Brewster scowled at Corey and me as if she knew exactly what we'd been doing. We both edged away from her sharp eyes.

Tracy shook her head. "Laugh if you want, but there was something in the dark watching me." Her voice dropped so low I could hardly hear her. "It wasn't Corey or Travis . . . or any other living soul."

Mrs. Brewster picked a stray blue napkin out of a pile of white tablecloths and waited for Tracy to go on. But Tracy just stood there, twisting her apron and trying not to cry.

"Is that all?" Mrs. Brewster sounded disappointed.

Tracy nodded. Tears ran down her face, and she wiped them away with her apron. "You wouldn't say 'Is that all' if you'd been there."

Mr. Brewster entered the kitchen as quietly as a ghost himself and frowned at us all, even Mrs. Brewster. "Leave the girl be," he said. "Can't you see? She don't want to talk about it."

With a sigh, Mrs. Brewster picked up an armful of tablecloths and headed for the laundry room. "Bring the napkins," she told Tracy, "and help me get the wash started."

As Tracy walked past, I grabbed her arm. "I know just what you mean," I told her. "Something's in the grove. I've felt it, too."

Corey nodded. "It's a scary place."

Although we hadn't spoken loudly, Mr. Brewster said, "If I was you, I'd stay away from there. No sense looking for trouble."

"What do you mean?" I asked.

He hesitated, hands deep in his pockets, chin stuck out.

"Trouble finds folks who look for it." Then, without another word, he left the kitchen. A moment later, we saw him walking toward the vegetable garden, pushing a wheelbarrow.

Corey made a face at his back and darted out the back door. I followed her. As we walked along the hedge separating the vegetable garden from the lawn, we heard Mr. Brewster say, "I thought you was doing the laundry."

"Tracy can do it," Mrs. Brewster said.

Peeking through the hedge, we watched her sit down on a bench. Mr. Brewster leaned on his hoe beside her, the weeding forgotten.

"Bound to be trouble now," he muttered.

"It's those grandchildren," Mrs. Brewster said. "Soon as I saw 'em, I knew they'd stir things up. Bad ones—that's what they are. I can spot 'em every time. They've got her up and about. And the little ones, too."

Mr. Brewster nodded, his face glum. "They wake up easy."

"And it's so hard to lull them back to sleep, poor dears."

"Mrs. Brewster!" Tracy called. "There's something wrong with the washer. Soap's everywhere. I can't shut it off!"

Mrs. Brewster shook her head. "Yep, things are stirred up, for sure. Next it'll be the lights and the TV and the plumbing."

"They'll keep me busy." Mr. Brewster sighed. "Not a moment's peace, that's for certain."

Mrs. Brewster got to her feet. "Better come with me," she said, "and take a look at the washing machine."

Mr. Brewster grunted to himself and laid down his hoe. "Weeds can wait, I reckon."

Corey and I crept away to the terrace behind the house and sat down at a table almost hidden by wisteria.

"What were they talking about?" I asked. "*Who* did we wake up?"

"They must be nuts or something," Corey said. "Blaming us when all we did was play a few pranks."

"It's not fair. We're not bad." A wasp settled down to explore a smear of jam on the table. I swatted it away absent-mindedly. "They act like it's our fault the washing machine broke."

The wasp landed on the table again. Corey watched it probe the jam, her forehead wrinkled as if she was memorizing its shape and color, its legs, its wings. It wasn't like my sister to be quiet so long.

At last, she looked at me, her face full of worry. "Maybe they think we woke up the ghosts. The ones that used to be here."

I stared at her. "But we faked it."

Corey shook her head. "We didn't fake what scared Tracy, and we didn't fake what scared you and me. Something's in the grove—and the Brewsters think we stirred it up." She glanced at the wasp. "Like we poked a stick in a hornets' nest, and they all flew out."

I glanced over my shoulder at the grove and felt the hair on my arms prickle. Part of me wanted to say "Don't be ridiculous," but another part of me was scared she was right.

Corey clasped her hands, twisting her fingers until her knuckles turned white, a worried frown on her face.

"What if we did, Travis?" she asked in a voice so low I had to lean close to hear her. "What if we did?"

"If we woke something up," I said, "let's hope Chester Coakley and Miss Duvall can put it back to sleep."

Corey got to her feet. "He should be here by now."

We came around the corner of the inn just in time to see a dusty black hearse pull into a parking place. KEEP THE DEAD PEACEFUL was painted on its side in large white Gothic letters, and underneath, in smaller letters was:

CHESTER COAKLEY
PSYCHIC INVESTIGATOR
THE MAN TO CALL WHEN THINGS GO BUMP

The license plate said, I C B-YOND.

The driver's door swung open, and out stepped a tall, thin man with a long gray ponytail and matching beard. He wore a Grateful Dead baseball cap, black jeans, and black boots. His faded black T-shirt said, I SEE—AND I CATCH—DEAD PEOPLE.

From the porch came a cry of delight. Clothing aflutter, Miss Duvall hurried down the steps and threw her arms around the man, almost knocking him flat on his back.

Chester Coakley had arrived.

The Jennings gang poured out of the inn and raced across the grass, calling out greetings. As Miss Duvall introduced them, they formed a respectful circle around Chester Coakley.

Catching sight of Corey and me, Miss Duvall beckoned to us. "Come and meet Chester."

Chester regarded us with the saddest eyes I'd ever seen.

His face was long and narrow, and his brow was carved with deep lines. He shook our hands and in a melancholy voice said, "Eleanor has told me all about you."

Turning to Corey, he added, "You are a sensitive, I hear."

For the first time, Corey seemed a little uneasy about her newly acquired psychic powers. With a shrug, she backed away from him.

"Don't be so modest!" Miss Duvall engulfed Corey in a smothering hug. To Chester, she said, "This little girl has witnessed several psychic manifestations. Indeed, I believe she's the catalyst for everything that's happened."

Chester nodded. "The catalyst. Of course. The one who sets everything in motion."

Miss Duvall returned her attention to Corey. "You see, dear, ghosts will not manifest unless someone sensitive to their presence is nearby. Obviously, the inn's previous owners were sensitives, like you. When they left and your very rational grandmother arrived, the ghosts became dormant. Now you're here, and they're once more on the prowl."

Corey shook her head, clearly alarmed.

"Don't be frightened," Miss Duvall said softly. "You have a great gift."

"No," Corey said. "It was a—"

I think Corey would have confessed everything if Grandmother hadn't arrived just then and interrupted her.

Barely concealing her dislike for the newcomer and his vehicle of choice, she gave him a teacher look that once must have terrified her students. "Mr. Chester Coakley, I assume?"

Chester gave a little bow and removed his baseball cap. "At your service, Mrs. Donovan."

Grandmother didn't return his smile. "I've given you a room on the second floor. Would you like to see it?"

"Sure—just give me a minute to grab my gear."

With obvious distaste, Grandmother watched Chester pull a tripod, strobe lights, and a camera bag out of the hearse. Miss Duvall took a crate of recording equipment and trudged into the inn behind Chester and Grandmother. The Jennings gang traipsed through the door after them, leaving Corey and me alone in the driveway.

"What a pair of nut cases." Hoping for a laugh, I tried to imitate Miss Duvall and Chester. "Oh, she's a catalyst, there has to be a catalyst."

Corey didn't even smile. Without a word, she turned her back on me and walked away.

"Where are you going?" I called after her.

"To my room. I want to be alone for a while."

I watched her go, hair swinging, shoulders squared, obviously upset. "Don't be stupid," I shouted. "You aren't a catalyst. They're crazy—and so are the Brewsters!"

But she kept going. Didn't look back. Didn't slow down. I could've run after her, but I knew it wouldn't do any good. When Corey got into one of her moods, you just had to wait until she got over it.

Not used to entertaining myself, I wandered around the grounds looking for something to do. I tried batting a tennis ball against the wall, but I kept missing it. I went inside and played a video game. I read a few pages of a Harry Potter book I'd already read three times. I started a crossword puzzle, but it was too hard.

Too lazy to put on my bathing suit and swim, I went back outside and walked through the garden to the place where I'd found the row of stones. I stared down at them, still puzzled.

Suddenly, a shadow fell across the weeds. Mr. Brewster stood a few feet away, blocking the sun. "What are you doing here?"

From the way he said it, you would've thought I'd climbed over a fence and trespassed on his own private land.

Instead of answering his question, I asked him one of my own. "What are these stones for? Why do they have numbers on them?"

He studied me as if I were a subspecies of the human race that should be extinct by now. "There's copperheads round here. Lots of 'em. Best stay away lest you get bit."

I looked at the mass of weeds and brambles growing over everything. Mr. Brewster had a point. It was snake territory, for sure.

I followed him back to the inn. "You didn't answer my question."

"You didn't answer mine," he said.

"But don't you wonder about those stones? Somebody went to a lot of trouble to line them up and write numbers on them."

"Whoever done it's dead and gone." Mr. Brewster stopped and scowled at me from under his bushy eyebrows. "Told you before. Leave things be that don't concern you."

With that, he walked a little faster, as though he was anxious to get rid of me. I slowed down and let the gap between us widen. Grumpy old man. Grandmother should fire both of the Brewsters. Surely she could find a good-natured hired man and a cook even better than Mrs. Brewster—people who might smile once in a while.

Although—or maybe because—Miss Duvall and Chester were looking for her, Corey stayed in her room until dinner.

I knocked on her door once, but she told me to go away. "I'm reading," she said.

"Is it a good book?" I asked.

"Yes."

"What's the title?"

"Go away."

I took her advice and left without even making a joke about a book called *Go Away*. In her present, very bad, mood, Corey wouldn't have been amused.

By dinnertime, the inn was full, and Tracy had to rush from table to table, taking orders, bringing food, and refilling water glasses.

Miss Duvall and Chester were holding forth at the Jenningses' table, describing their methods of discovering and recording ghostly presences.

Grandmother gave Chester a dark look. "Imagine a grown man driving around in a hearse, pretending to be a ghost hunter. Surely he can't earn a living doing that." She sighed. "Then again, maybe he can. Some people will believe anything."

For once, Corey had nothing to say. Still in her mood, she sipped her water and poked at the food on her plate, rearranging it instead of eating it.

"You're very pale," Grandmother said to her. "Do you feel all right?"

Corey shrugged. "I'm fine. Just not hungry."

Across the room, Chester's voice rose. "I tell you, the little girl's responsible. It's the same with poltergeists. They feed off the psychic energy of young people. Especially if the child is disturbed."

Chester had lowered his voice somewhat, but all three of us heard his last comment.

Corey looked at Grandmother, alarmed. "I'm not disturbed," she whispered.

Grandmother opened her mouth to speak, but I was too fast for her. Thinking to turn Chester's words into a joke, I said, "Of course you're disturbed, I've known that since the day Mom brought you home from the loony bin."

Grandmother stared at me, her face stern with anger. "That wasn't funny, Travis. Can't you see your sister's upset? Apologize for your insensitivity."

Before I had a chance to say anything, Corey jumped up from the table so hastily she overturned her chair. Without a word, she fled from the room.

Chester turned to us in dismay. "I'm so sorry," he said, "I didn't mean Corey's disturbed, I just—"

Grandmother rose to her feet with all the dignity of thirty years of teaching and stared the man down. "Please refrain from discussing the supernatural in Corey's presence. And mine and Travis's as well. This is our home, not a boardinghouse for ghosts."

With that, she hurried after my sister.

Tracy broke the embarrassed silence by entering the room with the dessert cart. Unaware of what had just happened, she moved among the tables, describing the evening's choices: apple pie à la mode, peach upside-down cake, crème brûlée, and "Death by Chocolate."

I guess if Tracy hadn't come along with the cart, I might have run after Grandmother and Corey, but who can turn down the world's best chocolate cake? Not me.

No sooner had I taken the first bite than Chester and Miss Duvall joined me. "Do you mind?" Chester asked as they sat down.

Of course I minded, but I was too polite to say so. Wimp that I was, I swallowed my mouthful of cake and smiled.

"Is your sister all right?" Miss Duvall asked. "Chester didn't mean to hurt her feelings. He was speaking in general of children who cause psychic manifestations, especially poltergeist activity."

"I don't suppose Corey has a history of shaking beds, broken furniture, loud noises, flying objects, rappings and tappings, and so on?" Chester asked.

"My sister is *not* disturbed." I glared at the man, sitting there in his dopey cap, wearing his dopey T-shirt. Suddenly, I hated him and his gray ponytail and his hearse. I decided to tell him the truth—maybe he'd go away and take the Jennings gang with him. If these were the kind of guests who came to the inn to see ghosts, I'd like to see the end of them.

"Corey's not psychic," I said in a voice loud enough for everyone in the dining room to hear. "If you want to know the truth, she and I—"

Before I could confess, Miss Duvall interrupted me. "I am so sorry, Travis. Chester has an unfortunate habit of asking thoughtless questions."

Here she broke off and scowled at Chester. He merely

shrugged and leaned back in his chair, grinning in such a vacant way I wondered if he was on some kind of medication.

"As for Corey's psychic powers," she went on to me, "I've been in this field long enough to recognize the real thing."

I laughed. "You're wrong. Corey and I faked everything."

Miss Duvall gave me a long, thoughtful look. "No," she said. "You and your sister may have begun this as a game, but the ghosts are awake now. Putting them back to sleep will not be easy."

A twinge of alarm raced across my scalp. "Putting them back to sleep will not be easy" echoed Mrs. Brewster's words from this morning a little too closely. Suppose everyone was right, and we actually *had* woken the ghosts of Fox Hill?

I must have kept my fear to myself, for Miss Duvall got to her feet and beckoned to Chester. "We have equipment to set up in the grove."

"You and your sister are welcome to join us," Chester said.

"Thanks," I said. But no thanks. Watching them leave the room, I told myself they were crazy. But an annoying little voice whispered, "What if they're not?"

7

The Jennings gang followed Miss Duvall and Chester, twittering about the grove and what they might see.

Mrs. Jennings paused and smiled at me. "I know you're a skeptic, Travis, but I hope you and Corey will join us tonight. Eleanor is convinced we'll have a better chance of seeing the ghost if your sister's with us."

"Don't count on it," I told her.

Mrs. Jennings sighed. "Chester was very tactless at dinner, but then I suppose that's how it is when you're a genius. The ordinary rules don't apply." With another smile and a pat on my shoulder, she hastened after the others, leaving a trail of sickeningly sweet perfume behind her.

Across the room, Tracy cleared tables. The setting sun shone through the windows and backlit her hair, making it shine like fine threads of gold.

She turned and caught me staring at her. "What do you think of Chester and Eleanor?" she asked.

"Bona fide nut cases, both of them."

With a serious face, she set her heavy tray on my table. "If you'd been in the grove last night, you wouldn't sound so smug."

More embarrassed than smug, I scraped the last bit of chocolate icing from my plate and licked it off my fork, tine by tine. "It's all fake," I said. "Corey and I wanted to make people think the inn was haunted so Grandmother would get more guests. She dressed up like a ghost and—"

Tracy shoved her face so close to mine we were almost nose to nose. Which would have been a thrill if she hadn't been so mad. "*There was something in the grove last night*—and it wasn't Corey!"

She snatched up my plate and fork, dumped them on her tray with a clatter, and huffed out of the dining room.

There I was, all by myself, surrounded by empty tables covered with dirty linen and crumpled napkins. It was obvious Tracy was never going to be my girlfriend. Not only was I tactless and offensive, but I was shorter and younger than she was.

"It was your imagination," I called after her, but the only answer I got was the *whop, whop, whop* of the kitchen door swinging back and forth.

"But what if it wasn't?" the little voice asked, a little louder this time. "What if . . . What if . . . ?"

Exasperated, I tossed my napkin on the table and went to find Corey. I wished we'd never thought of the ghost game.

As it turned out, Corey agreed with me. I finally found her sitting on the patio in the dark all by herself. At first she refused to look at me or answer any questions.

"Why are you mad at me?" I asked her. "What did I do?"

She turned to face me. "I told you I wanted to read, but you made funny noises outside my door, threw apples at my window, and thumped on my wall. You even unplugged my light and my radio and changed the time on my clock."

I stared at her. "Are you crazy? I knocked on your door once, and you told me to go away and I did. I never made funny noises or threw apples or thumped on your wall or anything."

"Then who did? Mr. Brewster?"

"Corey, I swear to you I did not do that stuff."

"Oh," she said sarcastically, "then it must have been the ghost."

We looked at each other in the moonlight, electrified by the same thought.

"No joke," I whispered.

"No." Corey folded her arms across her chest and shivered. "No joke."

Delicate shadows from the wisteria vine patterned the table and Corey's face, shifting as the breeze blew. From somewhere in the darkness, an owl hooted and another answered. Much closer, I heard something that sounded like a muffled giggle.

"Did you hear that?" I whispered.

Corey shuddered. "A mouse," she said. "A cat, a bird. Nothing to be scared of."

"Admit it," I said. "You *are* scared—and so am I."

She shook her head stubbornly. "Speak for yourself." At the same moment, we heard a whispering sound in the bushes and then the giggle—louder this time, followed by an eddy of cold air that tousled my hair and then Corey's.

My sister jumped to her feet. "Let's go inside."

The two of us ran to the inn and dashed through the

kitchen door, sure we were being chased by an invisible gang of ghosts.

Mrs. Brewster was scrubbing the sink. She frowned when the screen door slammed shut. "What's the big rush?" she asked. "A person would think something was after you."

Neither Corey nor I knew what to say. We just stood and stared at Mrs. Brewster, wishing we were safely home in New York or even at Camp Willow Tree—anywhere but here.

"I thought you two were out there with them so-called psychics." She waved a hand in the direction of the grove, where flashlights bobbed about in the dark. "They're aiming to take pictures of things that don't want their pictures taken," she muttered.

Grandmother opened the door to her apartment and poked her head into the kitchen. "Corey and Travis," she said, "it's time you were in bed."

At that moment, the power went off, and the inn became totally dark and silent—no lights, no radios, no humming refrigerator. Not a sound.

"Go get Henry," Grandmother told Mrs. Brewster. "The power's out again. I meant to get the wiring checked the last time this happened."

Grandmother had no sooner lit a candle than we heard a commotion outside—shouts, screams, the sound of people running toward us as if they feared for their lives.

Tripping over each other in their haste to get inside, the Jennings gang poured into the kitchen. Behind them, Chester was yelling, "We got an image!"

Grandmother closed her eyes and shook her head. "I

don't believe this." In a louder voice, she repeated herself. "I do *not* believe this."

Someone giggled, and Grandmother glared at me, her face stern in the candlelight. "This isn't funny, Travis!"

"I didn't laugh."

The guests milled around the kitchen, stumbling over things in the darkness. "Why are the lights off?" Mrs. Jennings cried.

"Please turn them on," Mrs. Frothingham begged. "We've had a terrible scare."

"Serves you right, you silly old scaredy cat," someone whispered, causing an outburst of giggles.

"Travis, apologize at once!" Grandmother said, shocked.

"It wasn't me!"

"I don't care who said it," Mrs. Frothingham cried. "Just turn the lights back on."

"I'm sorry, but the power's off." Grandmother lit more candles. As the kitchen brightened, something scurried into the shadows, too quickly to be seen.

"I can fix tea," Grandmother offered.

Some wanted tea. Others wanted something stronger. Two or three wanted to leave the inn at once.

The only ones in need of nothing were Eleanor Duvall and Chester Coakley. They were ecstatic. Not only had they seen something, but they'd captured its image on video.

"See?" Chester showed us a grainy image in the camera's monitor. Whatever it was wore a long dress and its hair was loose, but its face was too blurred to make out any features.

"She came like a blast of cold air," Miss Duvall said. "Silent, not a sound, but emanating malice."

"You probably saw the strobes light up," Chester put in. "She tripped the wires like I hoped and triggered the camera. It's the best paranormal experience I've ever had—and the best footage I've ever shot. Or seen, for that matter."

Mrs. Jennings clutched her teacup with shaking hands. "I'm very glad you children were not with us," she quavered. "I'll never get another good night's sleep."

Her friends nodded and cooed to each other in soft, comforting voices. Mrs. Frothingham sobbed into a wineglass. The wives were done with ghosts. No one wanted to see another one. In fact, they wished they hadn't seen the one they just saw.

The husbands laughed and talked too loud, already beginning to doubt they'd really seen a ghost.

"The image on that videotape," Mr. Bennett said. "It was probably the strobe lights. They caused a glare in the camera lens or something."

"Trick photography," Mr. Frothingham declared. "Double exposures. Easy to fake."

Mr. Jennings was the only husband to disagree. "No, it was the real thing," he insisted, gulping down a glass of something that made him cough. "I'm glad I saw it, but I don't care to see another."

Just then, every light came on, almost blinding us with their brilliance. The refrigerator began humming, and the dishwasher started—even though it hadn't been running before the power failure. Radios and TVs all over the inn came on, blasting noise at top volume.

Mr. Brewster stood at the top of the basement steps looking gloomier than usual. "I went to the fuse box," he said, "but before I so much as touched it, the power come back."

"How odd," Grandmother said.

"Nothing odd about it, ma'am." Mr. Brewster shook his head. "They been stirred up good and proper now."

Without another word, he trudged out of the kitchen, accompanied by a giggle that earned me a dirty look from Grandmother. I shook my head in protest, but she'd already turned her attention to Mrs. Brewster.

"What on earth was he talking about?" Grandmother asked.

"You'll find out soon enough." Squaring her shoulders, Mrs. Brewster strode out the door behind her husband.

Clearly bewildered, Grandmother looked at the guests. "Has everyone gone crazy?"

Chester patted her shoulder. "It's the ghosts," he said. "I told you, the girl's a catalyst."

Grandmother shrugged Chester's hand off. "I want you and your equipment out of here tomorrow morning. We've had nothing but trouble since you and that woman showed up."

Taking Corey and me by our arms, Grandmother ushered us out of the kitchen. In the doorway, she paused. "Will someone please turn off the radios and the television? Or at least turn them down?"

Snapping off her own television and radio, Grandmother frowned at me. "I expect you to apologize to Mrs. Frothingham tomorrow. You were very rude."

"But, Grandmother, I didn't—"

Silencing me with a look, she said, "If you continue to lie to me, I shall be forced to call your parents." She opened her bedroom door. "I need a good night's sleep. Please don't disturb me." With that, she walked into her room and shut the door.

I followed my sister into her room and sat beside her on the bed. "She hates us," Corey said. "We'll have to go to summer school now."

I shook my head. "She's just upset. And you can't blame her. This has been a really weird night. Especially for someone who doesn't believe in ghosts."

Corey sighed. "I wish we knew what Mr. Brewster thinks we stirred up."

Before I could come up with an answer, the light went off and the bed began to shake. Back and forth, up and down, jolting us like a carnival ride, harder and faster. We tried to hold on to the headboard, but in seconds we were thrown to the floor with a loud, bone-jarring thud. Too stunned to move, we cowered together while invisible fingers pinched us and pulled our hair and tweaked our clothes.

"Stop it," Corey yelled at me. "You're hurting me, stop it!"

"*You* stop it," I shouted, pushing her away.

At that, the room's dark corners rang with laughter. The empty bed bounced as if a gang of kids were jumping on it. The radio blared from one end of the dial to the other, and the bedside lamp flashed on and off. The closet door opened and slammed shut, opened and slammed shut, over and over again. Things thudded and thumped all around us. A book hit me in the head. A picture fell, and the glass in the frame broke.

"Who are you?" I cried in a voice so high and shaky I hardly recognized it as mine. "What do you want?"

An outburst of laughter answered me. Somebody yelled a string of cuss words

"I told you to go to sleep!" Grandmother stepped into the room and gasped, her face pale with shock. "What on earth have you done? Have you gone crazy?"

The closet door lay on the floor, the wood splintered from the hinges. Corey's clothes were scattered everywhere, some no more than ripped rags. Bureau drawers hung open, spilling their contents. Pages torn from books lay in drifts on the floor. Feathers from pillows still floated in the air. My sister covered her face with her hands and began to cry.

Grandmother stared at us as if we were monsters. "Why did you do this? What kind of children are you?"

"Bad children," a kid's voice whispered. "Lovely bad children!"

"What did you say?" Grandmother asked me.

"Nothing," I whispered. Out of the corner of my eye, I saw the shadows in the corner move, shifting the darkness from one place to another.

"It wasn't us," Corey sobbed. "We didn't do anything."

"Of course it wasn't the children." Chester peered over Grandmother's shoulder, grinning with apparent delight at the state of our room.

Grandmother whirled to face Chester, eager to take out her anger on him. "What are you doing here? This is my apartment, not part of the inn. Please leave at once!"

"Let him speak, Mrs. Donovan." Miss Duvall floated into the room on her tiny little feet, wearing her usual layers of filmy clothes. "Chester is the only one who can get to the bottom of this."

Her words caused an outburst of giggles from the corner. The same kid's voice whispered, "Fat bottom, fat bottom, fatty, fatty, fat bottom!" The giggles grew louder. Somebody said a rude word, which provoked even louder giggling.

Grandmother looked at Corey and me, alarmed for the first time. "Stop it," she ordered. "Or I'm sending you home tomorrow."

"Don't blame Travis and Corey," Chester said. "Can't you see they're just as scared as you are?"

"Ouch!" Miss Duvall began slapping at her rear end as if she were being pinched. "Stop it, stop it right now, you imps of Satan!"

The shadows raced around the walls, laughing and taunting her with insults relating to the size of her rear end.

Ignoring Miss Duvall, Grandmother looked at Chester as if she wished she could send him to the principal's office. "I am not scared!" she said, but the tremor in her voice gave her away.

"Old granny scaredy cat!" An invisible hand tugged at grandmother's sweater. "Nyah, nyah, nyah!"

Grandmother whirled around to stare at Corey, still crying on her bed, and me, sitting beside her. It was obvious we couldn't have been responsible for the tug on her sweater.

"Who did that?" she yelled. "What sort of tricks are you playing?"

For an answer she got a series of rude noises and a loud outburst of giggles, along with more cuss words.

While this was going on, Chester was aiming his camera at the corner where most of the noise came from. "Wow! Oh, wow!"

"Amazing manifestation," Miss Duvall whispered into her microphone. "Laughter, voices, poltergeist activity. My hair is standing up . . . the air is electrifying!"

Suddenly, a cold wind shot into the room. The curtains blew out straight from the windows, and the clothing and torn pages rose from the floor and spun around like tiny tornadoes. A low moan, almost a sob, rose from the corner. The shadows twisted and turned, now long, now short, and raced around the walls as if they were being chased.

Then the lights went out, and a harsh voice cried, "Enough! Back to where you belong. You will be punished for this!"

The moaning changed to high-pitched squeaks and yelps. Invisible hands pushed me out of their way, invisible feet stepped on mine, elbows poked my sides. The moonlight streaming through the window dimmed as shadowy shapes fled into the night, followed by something bigger and darker and far more terrifying.

After a sudden silence, the lights came on again. Torn clothing and shredded paper fell back to the floor. The curtains drooped. Whatever had been among us was gone.

Chester and Miss Duvall huddled together, elated by the activities they'd witnessed, but Grandmother sank down on the bed beside Corey and closed her eyes. My sister continued to sob.

I went to the window. The grove was a patch of inky

shadows on the moonlit grass. *"Who are you?"* I whispered. *"What do you want? Why are you here?"*

Nothing answered. Nothing stirred. A blanket of darkness lay over the earth, hiding everything. Shivering, I crept closer to Grandmother.

8

Miss Duvall was the first to break the unnatural silence. "Surely, Mrs. Donovan," she said in a theatrically low voice, "you can no longer harbor even the slightest doubt that the inn is haunted."

Grandmother raised her head and stared at the psychic. "Frankly," she said, "I don't know what to think."

"How else would you explain what we have all witnessed in this room?" Miss Duvall asked.

Grandmother rose to her feet, a little unsteadily, but with her dignity intact. "If you and Mr. Coakley are somehow responsible for this, I will bring a lawsuit against you."

Miss Duvall drew herself up as tall as possible and gave Grandmother a look of utter dismay. "I assure you that neither Chester nor I—"

Grandmother swept past as if the woman was of no more importance than a toadstool. "Please go back to your rooms," she said, "and do not enter my quarters again. By checkout time tomorrow, I expect you both to be gone."

"But—" Chester began.

"Nothing you can do or say will change my mind," Grandmother said. "I want you both out of here."

Turning to Corey and me, she added, "As for you two, please go to bed at once. We'll talk about this in the morning. I am exhausted."

Still protesting, Chester and Miss Duvall followed

Grandmother out of the room. "Don't you understand what this means to paranormal research?" Chester said.

Grandmother shut the door, and we didn't hear her answer.

"Please don't leave me here by myself, Travis," Corey begged. "I'm scared to death they'll come back."

She tossed me a blanket and an extra pillow, and I tried to make myself comfortable on the floor. I didn't want to be alone any more than my sister did.

"I kind of wish Grandmother *would* send us home," Corey said. "I don't like it here anymore."

"Even camp doesn't seem so bad now," I said. "Swimming in a freezing lake at seven A.M., eating lumpy oatmeal and mystery meat and mushy lima beans, hiking ten miles uphill."

"Making potholders and clay animals, singing those dumb camp songs, striking out in softball. . . ." Corey's voice slowed and thickened and finally trailed off in a sleepy mumble.

I turned this way and that, but whether I lay on my side or my back or my stomach, I couldn't relax. Every sound frightened me—a rustle in the leaves, a sigh of wind, the tap, tap of a branch against the window, a creak in the hall outside the door.

At any moment I expected to hear giggles and feel the pinch of invisible fingers. Worse yet, what if the thing from the grove came howling through the window again?

Early in the morning, I left Corey sleeping and hobbled back to my room, as stiff as an old man from sleeping on the floor.

Pages from books littered the floor, my favorite sweatshirt was now sleeveless, my T-shirts were torn in half, shreds of my socks hung from the ceiling light. My chair lay on its back on top of my desk, which was now on my bed. The mirror over the bureau was cracked, and the bureau's drawers were on the lawn, their contents scattered on the grass.

"Wow, what a mess." Chester stood outside my window, staring into my room.

Before I knew what he was doing, he'd climbed over the sill. "Mind if I take some pictures? This should be documented."

"Help yourself," I said. "Maybe you'd like to clean it up when you're done."

Chester laughed as if I were joking and began shooting. "The socks are a nice touch," he said, aiming his camera at the ceiling light.

Corey appeared in my doorway and glared at Chester. "Why are you still here?"

"We've got until noon to check out." Chester moved to my bed and photographed the desk and the chair from several angles "This is amazing stuff! Poltergeist activity, laughter, pinching, cussing, cold spots—I'll be the envy of every paranormalist in the world!"

"What are you doing in here?"

Grandmother took Chester by surprise. Clasping his camera to his chest, he backed away. "The children invited me in," he lied. "They—"

"Well, I'm *dis*inviting you," Grandmother said. "Get out of my grandson's room!"

"Yes, ma'am. I was just leaving anyway." Chester left the way he'd come in.

Grandmother looked around. "Please explain what's going on," she said in a weary voice. "If you can, that is."

"You were in Corey's room last night," I said. "You saw what we saw, you heard what we heard. I wish we could explain it, but . . ." I shrugged, unable to think of anything else to say.

Grandmother removed the chair from the desk, set it on the floor, and, with a sigh, sat on it. Shutting her eyes, she took a deep breath. "That's right. I saw, and I heard. As a result, I lay awake for hours trying to think of an explanation. And failed. Utterly."

Rising to her feet, Grandmother said, "I suggest we have breakfast. After that, please clean up your room. When everything is back to normal, I'd like to pretend last night did not happen."

Turning my back on the wreckage, I followed Grandmother to the dining room. She could chase off the psychics, she could make me clean up my room, she could pretend last night hadn't happened—she could even send Corey and me back to New York—but the ghosts were here, and they weren't leaving.

Not until they got what they wanted . . . whatever that was.

9

After breakfast, most of the guests checked out in support of Chester and Miss Duvall. At least that's what they claimed. I had a feeling some of them had had their fill of ghosts and didn't want to spend another night at Fox Hill.

Grandmother watched them leave. "So much for ghosts bringing business to the inn," she said.

A few minutes later, the Kowalskis joined us on the porch.

"What on earth was going on last night?" Mrs. Kowalski asked. "Our TV and radio came on, as well as the lights."

"We heard a lot of commotion, too," Mr. Kowalski added. "People shouting and running up and down the steps. We came here for peace and quiet, not wild parties."

Grandmother sighed. "I apologize for the disturbance. It won't happen again. The guests who were responsible are leaving today"

"It was that strange man with the hearse, wasn't it?" Mrs. Kowalski asked.

"And his bizarre lady friend." Her husband shook his head. "Crazy as loons, the pair of them. Going on and on about ghosts. What a load of hooey."

Mrs. Kowalski ran a hand through her short gray hair.

"Those two should get some exercise and clear their minds. Yoga would help. So would an organic diet."

Rackets in hand, the Kowalskis headed for the tennis court, and Grandmother turned to Corey and me. "Time to get some exercise yourselves," she said. "Go clean your rooms."

It took us all morning to sort through the wreckage. It was clear we'd need new clothes. New books, too—the pages of our summer reading books were scattered everywhere. Corey's favorite teddy bear had been torn limb from limb and his stuffing strewn on the floor.

I left Corey weeping over the bear and went outside to retrieve my bureau drawers. While I was gathering what was left of my underwear, I saw Mr. Brewster watching me.

"Don't expect no pity from me." He spat in the grass and started to walk away.

"Wait." I hurried over and stepped in front of him. "Please tell me about the ghosts."

"Get out of my way, boy." He tried to step around me, but I blocked him, as though we were playing basketball.

"Mr. Brewster, I have to know what they want, so I can make them go away."

For the first time I heard him laugh—a sort of growl combined with a cough. "They been here afore you, and they'll be here after you."

"But what are they? *Who* are they?"

The man sighed and wiped his forehead with an old handkerchief. "It woulda been best if them Cornells had never seen this house. Never bought it. Never fixed it up." He seemed to be talking more to himself than to me. "Some places ought to go to ruin. Let the bricks fall and the grass grow over them. Let it all be forgot and the dead stay dead."

With that, he stepped around me and headed toward the inn.

I stood where I was, cold despite the sun's heat, and watched him walk away. Then I gathered up the bureau drawers and their ruined contents and carried them back to my room.

Just before noon, the service bell rang. Grandmother rose from her chair with a sigh, laid her book aside, and headed for the office. Corey and I followed her inside. Surrounded by their luggage and gear, Chester and Miss Duvall were waiting to settle their bill.

Ignoring the couple's greeting, Grandmother sat down at the computer and looked up their account. As the bill was printing, she frowned. "I would appreciate your saying nothing about last night's events," she said.

"Oh, I can't agree to that, ma'am," Chester said. "I've already e-mailed my associates with the details. And spoken to my editor at *Chronicles of the Dead*."

"This sort of story simply cannot be swept under the rug," Miss Duvall added. "The public has a right to know."

"If you mention the name of this inn in a book or a magazine article or anywhere else," Grandmother said, "you will hear from my lawyer."

"But that's censorship," Chester put in. "You can't—"

"I can—and I will." Grandmother handed him the bill.

"That will be three hundred and seventy-seven dollars and five cents, including tax."

Chester slapped his credit card down on the counter, and Grandmother ran it through the machine. "Thank you," she said and handed the card back.

"But think of the free publicity," Miss Duvall said.

"I am," Grandmother said.

With a shrug, Miss Duvall swept out of the inn behind Chester. We watched the ghost hunter get into his hearse and drive away, with the psychic close behind in her VW.

"I feel better already," Grandmother said.

At lunchtime, the nearly empty dining room was so quiet I could hear bees buzzing in the flower boxes at the windows. The Kowalskis had ordered a box lunch and were off hiking in the hills, toting binoculars, bird books, cameras, and plenty of sunscreen.

Tracy came to our table to refill our glasses. "I hear you had a lot of trouble last night." Her hand shook as she spoke, and she spilled a few drops of water.

Grandmother watched her daub at the puddle with a corner of her apron. "Oh, leave it," she said impatiently. "Water won't stain anything."

"Sorry." Tracy stepped back from the table. "I don't know what's wrong with me. I just feel so nervous all the time. Everything makes me jump." Her eyes roved the room, lingering in the corners.

"We're all a little edgy," Grandmother said. "But now that those so-called psychics are gone, I'm hoping things will return to normal. Two guests are checking in this afternoon, and another three tomorrow. They asked about bike trails and hiking paths, shopping, historic sights—that sort of thing. Not one of them mentioned an interest in ghosts."

Tracy didn't seem to be listening. "I keep seeing things out of the corner of my eye," she said in a low voice. "But when I look straight at them, they're gone."

"That's just your imagination working overtime," Grandmother said.

Twisting her apron, her face red, Tracy said, "I called my mother this morning and told her about all the weird stuff. She said maybe I should come home."

Grandmother stared at her. "Tracy, didn't you hear what I just said? We have five reservations. You can't quit. I need you."

"I didn't say I was quitting," Tracy whispered. "I just said my mother thinks I should come home."

"And what do *you* think?" Grandmother asked. "You're sixteen years old. Surely you have your own opinions."

"Yes, ma'am, of course I do." Tracy's eyes got watery, and her lower lip quivered. I wanted to leap up and defend her, perhaps throw my arms around her and protect her, but I just sat there like a nincompoop.

"Well?" Grandmother asked, her voice softening at the sight of a tear rolling down Tracy's cheek. "Will you stay and help me?"

Tracy wiped her eyes with her hands. "I'll stay," she said, ". . . as long as the ghosts don't come back."

If I hadn't felt so sorry for her, I would have remined her of what she'd said before she did her Nancy Drew act in the grove—"I'm not afraid of anything."

"I don't expect any more manifestations," Grandmother said. "Not with that lunatic and her crazy companion out of the picture."

"Do you really think Mr. Coakley and Miss Duvall faked the whole thing?" Tracy asked.

"I don't know how they did it, but I'm sure they were responsible."

I glanced at Corey. She sat quietly, poking her salad this way and that in an effort to make it look as if she'd eaten some of it. She'd been so quiet all day I was beginning to worry about her.

"I hope you're right, Mrs. Donovan." Tracy's eyes returned to the corners of the room, as if she'd just glimpsed something moving in the shadows.

"A man who wears a ponytail and drives around in a hearse is simply not to be trusted." Grandmother ate the last of her sandwich and got to her feet. "Neither is a woman over twenty who polishes her nails black, pierces her nose and heaven knows what else, and claims to have psychic powers."

With that, she left the dining room, her faded denim skirt swinging.

Tracy sat down at our table and rested her chin on her hands. "If your grandmother didn't need me, I'd leave right now." She tried to pour herself a glass of water, but this time it slopped all over the table.

"Clumsy," someone whispered.

"What did you say?" Tracy turned to me.

"I didn't say anything."

"Clumsy, sloppy girl."

Tracy jumped up and whirled around, trying to see

who'd spoken. Her apron slid to the floor, its strings untied, and the same giggling we'd heard last night rippled around the room. Here and there, a cloth slithered off a table, forks, spoons, and knives rose into the air, and napkins whirled like eddies of leaves on a windy day. China plates and cups smashed against walls. Ketchup bottles spurted like ruptured arteries and splattered tables and carpets.

The three of us cowered together, our flesh pinched, our hair pulled, our faces slapped by invisible hands, until we screamed.

With a bellow of rage, Mrs. Brewster barreled into the room, her chest heaving. "Behave, bad ones, behave!" she screamed.

"It's not us," I yelled. "We didn't do anything!"

But it wasn't us Mrs. Brewster was looking at. Her eyes were focused on the swinging chandelier. "Stop it this minute!"

Behind her, a pitcher of water rose from a table, sailed through the air, and dumped itself on the old woman's head. The giggles changed into wild laughter. A cold draft swirled around us. Giving us a few last pinches, something swept out of the room.

Tracy ran to Mrs. Brewster and began drying her with a tablecloth. "Are you all right?"

Mrs. Brewster pushed Tracy aside and surveyed the dining room. "One of you fetch Mr. Brewster," she said. "Tell him it's worse than before."

As I ran out of the room to find Mr. Brewster, I bumped into Grandmother rushing into the room.

"No," she cried. "I don't believe this!"

"I want my mother," Tracy wailed.

Leaving them to settle things, I dashed out the back door and began searching for Mr. Brewster. I found him weeding the vegetable garden.

"Mrs. Brewster sent me to get you," I shouted. "She says it's worse than before!"

The old man dropped the hoe and came running. He didn't ask for an explanation. He knew.

"So they done all this," he said glumly, taking in the dining room. Overturned chairs, linens on the floor, puddles of water, broken china, ketchup on the walls, Tracy weeping, his wife rubbing her wet hair with a tablecloth.

Turning to Corey, Mr. Brewster added, "You and your pranks. I hope you're satisfied, miss."

Without looking at him, my sister ran out of the dining room. When I followed her, she tried to slam her door in my face, but I managed to push my way into her room.

"What's wrong with you?" I yelled. "Why won't you talk to me? Are you mad at me?"

"I'm scared," she whispered. "Just scared. That's all." She sank down on her bed and began to cry. "I want to go home."

I sat beside her and patted her shoulder. "Don't you think I'm scared, too?"

"Let's call Mom."

"No." My chest was so tight with fear I thought I was having a heart attack. "We started this, and we have to finish it."

Corey raised her head and looked at me with teary eyes. "But how do we do that?"

"They're ghosts," I said. "They must be here for a reason. Unfinished business or something."

"The Brewsters know more than they're saying," Corey muttered.

As she spoke, I glanced out the window and saw Mrs. Brewster walking slowly across the grass toward the barn. Her hair and dress were still wet from the pitcher of water. She looked tired. While I watched, she vanished behind the hedge.

"I wonder where she's going," I said.

Corey perked up. "Let's follow her."

We ran across the lawn and peeked through the hedge. Mrs. Brewster was standing in the weeds, staring down at the numbered stones. "It's too bad, that's what it is," she said softly. "You ought to be sleeping peaceful. All of you."

As she spoke, shadows stirred among the stones and whispered in the grass.

"That boy and girl are bad ones," she muttered, "full of pranks and mischief, just like you."

She cocked her head like a robin listening for a worm to turn in the earth. "No, it ain't punishment they need," she said. "No more than you needed it."

She cocked her head again, listening hard to the rustle in the weeds, and then looked up, straight at our hiding place. "Come out from there. Didn't nobody teach you manners?"

Corey and I stepped through a gap in the hedge. A cloud drifted across the sun and turned the day cold.

"Who were you talking to?" I whispered.

"Nobody." Mrs. Brewster frowned at Corey and me, her face grim.

"You were talking to *them*." Corey's voice shook. "They're here, I can feel them all around us, watching, listening."

Hoping to calm her, I took my sister's hand, but she snatched it away. "Tell us who they are," she cried. "Tell us what they want! Tell them we're sorry. Tell them—"

"'Sorry' can't change nothing," Mrs. Brewster interrupted. "It's got to run its course now."

"But can't you just tell us who they are?" I asked.

"I can't," Mrs. Brewster said, "but maybe *they* will." With that, she pushed past us and strode off toward the inn. Even her shadow looked angry.

For a moment, I thought Corey was going to run after her and keep begging for answers, but she stayed where she was, head down, staring at the numbered stones.

"Come on." I reached for her hand again. "Let's go back to the inn."

The cloud had moved past the sun, and the day was hot again, thick with humidity and buzzing, biting bugs.

Corey watched a butterfly drift from one stone to the next, pausing to fan its wings. "I never really believed in ghosts before," she said.

"Me, either."

As I spoke, a pebble hit my cheek, then another and another. Suddenly, the air was full of pebbles, striking Corey and me but too small to do more than sting. At the same moment, the giggling started. And the whispers.

Corey and I ran toward the hedge, pebbles flying after us, but before we reached it, a shadow detached itself from the deep shade and blocked our path. Corey covered her face with her hands, but I stared into the darkness so hard my eyes stung. Someone was there, but I couldn't see more than a vague shape.

"Who are you?" I whispered.

"Who are you?" it whispered back, coming a little closer.

"What do you want?"

"What do you want?"

"Stop copying me!"

"Stop copying me!" it yelled in a shaky voice just like mine. "Stop copying me, stop, stop."

Laughter erupted all around us. A hand pulled my hair so hard I saw strands floating away.

Corey cried out in pain and stumbled backward, holding her cheek, the skin red from a slap.

"You'd better be scared," someone whispered. "We're the bad ones, the lovely bad ones, the bad, bad, bad ones."

Corey and I ran, but we couldn't escape the laughter or the pinches, slaps, and yanks at our hair. It was like being chased by a swarm of stinging hornets. Only worse. When hornets sting you, you know what they are. You can see them.

Somewhere near the grove, our pursuers gave up and let us escape. But we kept running until we reached the inn and stumbled through the kitchen door.

Mrs. Brewster looked up from the chicken she was preparing and scowled. Before she could say a word, we rushed past her and headed for the library. Neither of us wanted another scolding.

10

We collapsed on a couch in the library, breathing hard and soaked with sweat, our skin dotted with red marks left by the pebbles. The afternoon sun slanted through the tall windows and lit the bookcases on the opposite wall. Dust motes floated in the columns of light. The air was quiet, undisturbed. The only sound was the drowsy hum of bees in the flower boxes.

In other words, everything felt normal. Ordinary. On the surface, at least.

Corey picked up an old *New Yorker*. She leafed through it, not even pausing to read the cartoons, then threw it aside.

As restless as my sister, I prowled around the room, studying the books on the shelves, wishing I could find something to read but knowing I was in no mood to sit quietly. Something was going to happen—I could sense it in the air like electricity before a thunderstorm.

Suddenly, a pamphlet slid off a shelf and fell to the floor at my feet. Corey gasped, but I picked it up and read the title—*The Strange History of Fox Hill, as Recorded by the Reverend William Plaistow.*

"*They* must have knocked it off the shelf," Corey whispered.

We looked around the room uneasily. The back of my neck prickled as if someone was watching me, but I heard no giggles or whispers and felt no slaps or pinches.

"They want us to read it," Corey said.

Cautiously, I opened the pamphlet. With Corey pressed close to my side, I began reading out loud.

"This treatise is dedicated to those who suffered at Fox Hill Poor Farm, especially, if I may borrow a few lines from John Greenleaf Whittier, the children:

The happy ones; and sad ones;
The sober and the silent ones; the boisterous and glad ones;
The good ones—Yes, the good ones, too;
and all the lovely bad ones."

"Poor farm?" Corey stared at me. "What's that?"

"It's where they used to send people who didn't have anywhere else to go."

"Like the workhouse in *Oliver Twist*?"

"Yes." I turned the page and went on reading.

"Built in 1778, Fox Hill Farm was originally the home of Jedediah Cooper. Unfortunately, Jedidiah's great-grandson, Charles Cooper, amassed enormous gambling debts, which made it impossible for him to pay his property taxes. After repeated warnings, the county seized the farm in 1819 and attempted to sell it at public auction. When no buyer stepped forth, the county put the property to use as a poor farm in 1821.

"Mr. Cornelius Jaggs was appointed overseer of the poor. He chose his sister, Miss Ada Jaggs, to supervise the children. These two ran Fox Hill for the next twenty years. Apparently, their harsh, perhaps even cruel, treat-

ment of the helpless people in their care eventually caused an outcry from the local populace. After a public hearing in 1841, the two were dismissed from their positions, and the poor farm was shut down.

"Cornelius Jaggs left the area at once and vanished into the fog of history. Deserted by her brother, Ada Jaggs hanged herself in a grove of trees not far from the house."

Corey and I looked outside at the grove. Even though there was no breeze, the leaves of the tallest tree stirred and its branches swayed. A bunch of crows rose into the air, cawing, and flew away as if something had disturbed them.

The page turned all by itself. A cloud drifted across the sun, and the dim light made it hard to read the faded print.

"Ada Jaggs is buried at Fox Hill, along with many poor souls who suffered and died on the farm.

"Among her dead companions are at least a dozen boys whom she singled out for her most severe punishments. Guilty of no more than normal high spirits, these boys, my lovely bad ones, had their lives cut short by a cruel and wicked woman."

The whisper I'd been expecting now ran around the walls. "Bad, bad, bad. *She* was the bad one. Bad beyond telling, bad beyond belief."

The whisper died away, but no one giggled. No one pinched or kicked or slapped. Sorrow filled the room. It pressed down on us, heavy and dark and so full of pain we could hardly breathe.

A cold hand touched my face. "Don't be afraid."

With Corey pressed against my side, I focused on the shadow standing in front of me. Slowly, a boy took shape, maybe ten or eleven years old, his face pale and freckled, his clothes ragged. He stood as straight and tall as he could and stared into my eyes.

"I'm Caleb," he said. "That's Ira, and Seth."

Two boys stepped out of the shadows. Ira was about the same age as Caleb, dark and melancholy. Seth was the littlest of the three, with a tangled head of red curls and two missing front teeth. I guessed he was about seven.

"There's more of us," Caleb said. "But we've been chosen to do the talking."

"I'm sorry we scared you," Ira said, "but—"

"I ain't sorry," Seth said. "We're the bad ones! We got to live up to our name."

Giggles ran along the shadowy walls like a stream running over pebbles, chuckling to itself. "Bad ones, bad ones, bad, bad, bad."

Speechless, Corey and I huddled together like scared sheep and stared at the boys—the ghosts, that is. The bad ones.

And they stared at us. Seth made a sudden lunge as if he meant to pinch us, and we scooted backward. The giggles got louder.

"What do you want?" Corey whispered.

"You woke Miss Ada up with your tomfoolery," Caleb said. "And she woke us up. Now you have to put us back to sleep."

"And her, too," Seth put in.

"So we can rest easy," Ira said. "Without her coming after us, over and over and over. Didn't she cause us enough grief when we were alive?"

"But—but how can we?" I stuttered and stammered, unable to say anything that made sense. "I mean, what can we do, we're just kids. We aren't—"

"I told you it wouldn't do any good to talk to them," Ira muttered to Caleb. "The living know nothing."

A whisper of mutterings swept around the room, from shadow to shadow. "Stupid, stupid, stupid," someone chanted. "Don't know nothing either one of you."

"Pinchy, pinchy, pinchy," someone whispered, plucking at my skin.

"Ouch, that hurts!" I shouted, trying to evade the invisible fingers.

"Stop it!" Corey flailed her arms as if she was trying to hit the shadows romping around us.

"Boys, boys," Caleb called. "Leave them be. They can't help being ninnies."

The voices whispered to themselves, but they withdrew to the corners of the room and sulked there.

"Pay the shadow children no mind," Ira said. "They don't mean any harm."

"Now," Caleb said to us, "you read about Miss Ada. I reckon you know she's in the grove."

Seth giggled. "You might say that's where she hangs out."

Caleb and Ira whirled to face Seth. "Hush your foolish mouth!" Caleb yelled. "Don't make mockery of her."

"Do you want her barging in here and hurting us again?" Ira asked.

Seth's mouth turned down, and he looked at the floor. "She don't come out till dark," he whispered. "She can't hear what we say in the daytime." He raised his head and looked at the older boys. "Can she?"

"She always had a wicked sharp ear," Ira said. "No telling what she can hear and when and where."

Caleb nodded. "So it's best not to go making jokes about her way of dying."

"She blames us for it," Ira said.

"She blames *you* for what *she* did to herself?" Corey asked.

"She's the blameful sort," Caleb said. "All that she did to us was our fault."

"We made her do it," Ira said.

"If we'd been good children, she'd have fed us cookies and milk," Seth said, "and put us to bed under blankets soft as clouds and warm as cats."

"But we was bad, baaaaad, baaaaad," the shadow children whispered.

"And so she punished us," Ira said. "For our own good."

"Even though it pained her most horribly to hurt us," Caleb added in a voice as sweet as the sweetest lie ever told.

"She loved the stick she beat us with," Ira muttered. "And that's the truth of it."

"She beat us for *her* good," Caleb agreed. "Not ours."

"Baaaaad, baaaaad," the shadow children hissed. "*She* was baaaaad."

"Badder than us," Seth said, "badder than the devil hisself."

Grandmother appeared in the doorway. "Corey and Travis, I've been looking all over for you. It's time for dinner."

It was clear she didn't see the bad ones. Caleb shrugged and grinned. "Like most folks, your grandma only sees what we *do*. She don't see *us*."

"Watch this." Without even taking a step, Seth was standing in front of Grandmother, waving and grinning at her. "Hi, there, Granny!"

Grandmother shivered. "It feels cold all of a sudden. Is the window open?"

Caleb frowned, but Seth giggled and kicked Grandmother's shin lightly—just a tap, really.

Puzzled, Grandmother stared around the room. "I could swear someone just kicked me, but—"

In a second, Seth was at the reading table. Grabbing a couple of magazines, he tossed them at Grandmother. They zoomed past her head and fluttered to the floor behind her.

"What in the world?" As Grandmother whirled to look at the magazines, Ira grabbed Seth's right arm and Caleb grabbed his left arm. All three vanished. A draft of cold air followed them past Grandmother and out the door.

"Did you see that?" Grandmother asked. "The wind blew those magazines right off the table." Her voice shook, but she crossed the room briskly and began closing the windows. "It must be the cold front the weatherman predicted."

As she shut the last window, the dark clouds I'd noticed earlier burst, and the wind drove sheets of rain against the glass.

"Looks like we're in for a bad storm." Grandmother led the way toward the dining room, thunder crashing and lightning flashing. "I hope we don't lose the power."

While we waited for our meal, I asked Grandmother if she knew the inn had once been the county poor farm.

"Poor farm?" She looked at me in amazement. "Whatever gave you that idea?"

I laid the pamphlet on the table. "I found this in the library."

She picked it up and read the title out loud. "My goodness, I went through all the books in the library when I bought Fox Hill, but I swear I never saw this."

Mrs. Brewster chose that moment to arrive with our dinner. "Where did you get that pamphlet?" she asked.

"Travis came across it in the library." Grandmother opened the pamphlet, her face puzzled. "Oh, what a pity. Most of the pages have fallen out."

Mrs. Brewster turned her sharp old eyes on me. "You just found it on the shelf, did you?"

"Well, actually, it sort of fell on the floor, and I picked it up," I muttered.

She set my plate in front of me. "They're telling you what they want you to know," she whispered. "Better pay heed."

Grandmother looked at Mrs. Brewster. "What was that?"

"Nothing. Just telling Travis he'd better eat that chicken before it gets cold. It's best ate warm."

With that, she set the rest of the plates down and crossed the room to take the Kowalskis' order.

"Where's Tracy?" Corey asked.

"Her mother came for her this afternoon," Grandmother said. "She promised she'd come back next week to help with a busload of senior citizens arriving on Monday. They'll be here three nights—twelve people. If she doesn't show up, I'll have to put you and Travis to work waiting tables and cleaning rooms."

Grandmother took a bite of chicken and glanced out the window at the dark clouds and flashing lightning. "I just don't understand how a sensible girl like Tracy can be so silly."

I heard a creaking sound and looked up. In the center of the ceiling, Caleb perched on the chandelier. Every now and then, he twirled it around, as if it were a swing. So far, no one but me had noticed the noise.

Ira opened and shut the door to the kitchen, making it appear as if the wind was doing it. Grandmother looked annoyed. "Henry will have to do something about that door," she said.

On the other side of the dining room, Seth stole Mrs. Kowalski's napkin. She asked Mrs. Brewster for another. He took that one, too. And the one after that.

"I've brought you three napkins," Mrs. Brewster snapped. "What are you doing with them?" She sounded as if she was accusing Mrs. Kowalski of stealing them.

Mrs. Kowalski looked offended. "I put them on my lap," she said, "but they keep disappearing. It's *very* peculiar."

Mrs. Brewster glanced around the room. To my amazement, she looked right at the chandelier where Seth now perched with Caleb. She frowned and shook her head at him. He stuck out his tongue and laughed.

"Stop it right now," she said crossly.

Corey kicked me under the table. "Mrs. Brewster *sees* them," she whispered. "She sees them!"

I nodded, too flabbergasted to speak.

In the meantime, Mrs. Kowalski was scowling at Mrs. Brewster. "Stop doing what?" she asked. "I told you I'm not doing anything with the napkins! They just keep—"

Mrs. Brewster tossed a napkin on the table and headed for the kitchen, her broad back stiff.

"That woman has no right to speak to me like that," Mrs. Kowalski told her husband. "*I* don't know where the napkins went."

Twittering to themselves, the shadow children gathered around the two new guests, Miss Baynes and Miss Edwards, who had checked in that afternoon. Unaware they were being watched, the old women sipped their iced tea and talked in low voices. Their hair was beauty-shop perfect, and their clothes were without creases or wrinkles.

Suddenly, the casement windows blew open, the chandelier spun round and round, and the kitchen door banged like a series of pistol shots. Thanks to Ira, Mr. Kowalski's coffee spilled, and Seth dropped a mouse on the old ladies' table. They screamed as it darted to the edge, ran down the tablecloth, and scurried across the floor.

It all happened so fast no one knew what to do first. Grandmother leapt up to close the windows. Mrs. Brewster came rushing out of the kitchen to mop up the coffee and bring Mr. Kowalski a fresh cup.

The old ladies were acting like comic-strip women,

screeching and turning this way and that in case the mouse made another foray.

"I've never seen a mouse in the dining room," Grandmother said, all aflutter with embarrassment.

"I'll make sure you don't never see another one," Mrs. Brewster muttered with a scowl at the chandelier where Caleb, Ira, and Seth sat grinning at her. "'Tain't funny, 'tain't funny a'tall."

"The health department would fail to see any humor in a mouse infestation," Miss Baynes agreed in a voice as frosty as her hair.

While Grandmother's attention was focused on Miss Baynes and Miss Edwards, Corey and I made a quick retreat to the lounge to watch television. We had no idea what the bad ones would do next, but we didn't want Grandmother to blame us for it.

11

Wielding the TV remote, I clicked through horror movies, nature shows, sitcom reruns, and dozens of commercials until I found a dumb comedy on HBO. We'd seen it before, but it was just the thing to take our minds off the ghosts. And to delay going to bed.

Just as we were getting interested in the movie, the scene suddenly changed. One minute, a bunch of rowdy teenagers were laughing it up at a party; the next minute, a pair of horses was pulling an old farm wagon along a muddy road in the country. It was almost dark. Rain poured down. The trees were bare. Mountains loomed against the sky, their tops hidden in clouds. There wasn't a house or a barn in sight. No livestock. No people. Just woods and fields and mud.

"Did you switch channels?" Corey grabbed the remote from me and clicked the number for HBO, but the scene didn't change. She tried TMC, MTV, CNN, ABC, PBS, even HTV. The horse and wagon was on every channel.

"Something must be wrong with the satellite dish," I said. "Maybe the wind or—"

I took the remote back and turned the TV off, but the movie stayed on. The driver hunched over the reins, soaked through. Behind him, a family huddled in the open wagon, heads down, wet, cold, miserable. The camera zoomed in on a sign clumsily lettered "County Poor Farm."

"Oh, my gosh!" Corey grabbed my arm. "It's Fox Hill!"

The camera shifted to the inn's front porch. A short, plump man stood there, watching the wagon approach. His face was round, but there was nothing jolly about his expression.

Beside him was a woman. Her face was pale and hard, her eyes small and close set under straight dark brows. She wore a long black dress, buttoned to her chin. She, too, stared at the wagon.

The man pulled out a pocket watch. "It's John Avery with the Perkins family, right on schedule." His voice was nasal, harsh, and unpleasant. "Four of 'em. Man and wife, baby girl, boy."

The woman frowned. "More shiftless folks for us to feed and shelter," she said with a sniff.

"I hear the boy's ill mannered," the man said. "No respect for his betters. Ungrateful. Surly. A bad one."

The woman's thin lips twitched up at the corners. "Once he's in my care, he'll change his ways."

The man glanced at her with approval. "You have never failed to break the spirit of the most rebellious child."

The wagon pulled up beside the porch. "All right, you lot," the driver said. "Ride's over."

Hauling their rain-soaked belongings in a couple of small sacks, the Perkins family climbed out of the wagon. The woman looked weak and frail, and the baby clung to her, its tiny hands gripping its mother's shawl.

The man helped his wife to the muddy ground, but he was almost as sickly as she was.

The camera zoomed in on the boy, showing every feature clearly—freckles, chipped front tooth, shaggy blond hair.

"Caleb," I whispered. "It's Caleb."

The short, plump man peered at Mr. Perkins. "You fit to work?"

"Yes, sir, Mr. Jaggs." A deep, hard-edged cough interrupted Mr. Perkins's answer. Somehow he controlled it and went on. "I'm fit. I'd still be working my own land if—"

"No excuses," Mr. Jaggs snapped. "I've heard so many pitiful stories it's a wonder I can sleep at night."

The family stood in a crooked row, soaked by the rain, all heads down save Caleb's.

Miss Ada turned to him. "You, boy," she said. "I don't care for the look in your eye."

Caleb shrugged. "There's much in this world I myself don't care for, ma'am. This place, to name one."

"How dare you speak to me with such insolence." Miss Ada struck Caleb across the face with her open hand.

He flinched, but I swear his eyes dared her to strike him again.

Mrs. Perkins gasped and stepped forward as if to shield Caleb. "I told you to mind your tongue, son."

Mr. Jaggs signaled to a burly man lurking near the steps. "Joseph, take the boy away."

"No," Mrs. Perkins said. "He's just a child, he didn't mean to be impudent."

Joseph ignored the woman. Grabbing Caleb's arm, he dragged him away.

At the same time, Mr. Jaggs summoned an old woman from the house. Gesturing to Caleb's mother, he said, "Show Mrs. Perkins to the women's quarters, Sadie. I'll see to Mr. Perkins."

"Please," Mrs. Perkins said, "let me stay with my husband."

Miss Ada raised an eyebrow and turned to Mr. Jaggs. "Mrs. Perkins must think she's a guest at a grand hotel. Perhaps she'd like a nice soft bed and a warm fire."

The old woman tugged at Mrs. Perkins's arm. "'Tis best you do as they say," she whispered. "The men's quarters are separate from the women's. You won't see much of your husband whilst you're here."

Pressing the baby close to her heart, Mrs. Perkins allowed the old woman to lead her away.

Head hanging, Mr. Perkins trudged off behind Mr. Jaggs. Even after he was out of sight, we heard him coughing.

The camera shifted to Joseph and Caleb. The man dragged the boy into a building behind the inn—the carriage house, I thought—and took him down a steep flight of stairs into a dark basement. Opening a heavy wooden door, he thrust Caleb into a small cell.

"Mebbe the rats will teach you to keep a civil tongue in your head." With that, he slammed the door shut and locked Caleb into a room that was smaller than a closet, maybe three feet by three feet. No way to lie down unless you curled yourself into a ball. Dirt floor. No window. No light. No heat. Not even a blanket.

Caleb hurled himself against the door and beat on it with his fists. He yelled, shouted, kicked. Exhausted, he finally gave up and sank down on his haunches.

The camera moved away from Caleb, out of the cell, out of the building, farther and farther until it seemed to be high in the sky looking down on Fox Hill and the farmland rolling away to the mountains. The scene slowly dimmed, and the screen went dark.

Alone in the silent room, Corey and I stared at the TV as if we were waiting for part two to begin. When nothing happened, Corey turned to me. "How did they do that?"

She meant the bad ones, of course. I shook my head. Too much had happened too fast for me to understand any of it.

While we sat there puzzled and scared, we heard Grandmother's footsteps in the hall. "What are you two doing, sitting in the dark?" she asked. "Is the TV broken?"

I got to my feet, aching with exhaustion. "We were just going to bed."

"Good," Grandmother said. "I was coming to tell you to do just that."

Corey yawned and followed me out of the guest lounge. At her bedroom door, she paused to whisper, "I don't want to see any more about the poor farm."

Then, without another word, she closed her door and left me in the dark hall.

I'd seen enough myself, but I had a feeling there was more, and, like it or not, we were going to watch it.

12

I hadn't been asleep long when I woke up freezing cold. Seth had yanked my covers off. He perched at the foot of my bed, laughing. Caleb bounced a ball against the wall over my head, and Ira rocked back and forth in the rocking chair.

"What?" I mumbled, still half asleep.

Seth giggled. "We ain't done with you yet."

I pulled the blankets toward me, as if it was the most natural thing in the world to deal with mischievous ghosts.

"Travis is cold," Ira observed.

"Cold—I scarcely 'member what that's like," Seth said.

"Being dead has its advantages." Caleb jumped to his feet and raised an arm in a theatrical gesture. "'Fear no more the heat o' the sun,'" he proclaimed. "'Nor the furious winter's rages.'"

"'Thou thy worldly task hast done,'" Ira added. "'Home art gone, and ta'en thy wages.'"

"Shakespeare," Caleb said. "We had to memorize it in school, back before we came here."

"Little did we know then," Ira said, his face suddenly sad, "how soon we'd 'come to dust.'"

"But we ain't cold and we ain't hot and we ain't hungry," Seth reminded them. "We done been put out of our misery, boys."

Caleb yanked my covers off again. "There's still much for you to learn."

Pulling a sweatshirt over my pajamas, I followed the bad ones to the door.

My sister stood in the hall with the shadow children. "They woke me up, too," she said glumly.

The TV was already on in the lounge. On the screen, a deep snow covered the ground, and a fierce wind roared in the trees. The camera led us to a brick building, gone now. Inside, the ceilings were low, the rooms small and cold and dark. The only heat rose through floor vents from a stove on the first floor. Wrapped in a thin blanket, Caleb's mother huddled on a narrow cot. She held the baby to her breast, rocking it gently. Two women sat nearby, as if trying to share the warmth of their bodies with her.

"She's dead," one woman whispered. "Let her go, there's naught more you can do."

"Poor little baby," the other whispered. "It's a cruel world, a wicked world with no mercy."

Caleb's mother didn't answer, nor did she give up the baby.

"Please, Sarah," the first woman begged. "Lay her aside. We'll see she has a proper burial."

"The good Lord has taken her," the second said, "to spare her suffering."

At last, Caleb's mother let the women have the baby. "He should have taken me," she whispered, "not her."

"He'll take us all soon enough," the first woman said.

The scene slowly faded, and a new image appeared. The men's quarters this time, as cold and bleak as the women's. Two men stood over a bed where a dead man lay. Caleb's father. Without a word, they moved the body to a board and covered it with a cloth. Picking it up, they carried it down the stairs and to the barn. The morning was gray, and the ground was muddy. The maples had begun to bud, and a blackbird sang a few notes.

"First his little daughter, then his wife," one man said. "All he had left was the boy."

The other man coughed. "And him none too well from the looks of him."

"No worse'n the rest of us."

Mr. Jaggs appeared at the barn door, and the man who had just spoken spat into the mud. "Should be *him* we're burying."

"And her, too," the other said as Miss Ada joined Mr. Jaggs.

Again the picture faded.

Corey and I looked at Caleb. "Your whole family died here?" I asked.

"And me, as well," he said.

"All of us." Seth waved his hand at Ira and the shadow children watching us from the corners.

"And many more," Ira added.

Images appeared on the TV, silent this time. Gaunt, ragged people lined up for watery soup and hard bread. They worked outside in pouring rain and wind, in the cold of winter and the heat of summer. They shivered in dark, cold rooms. They went coatless and barefoot in the snow. They coughed and wheezed and sickened and died.

And all the while, Mr. Jaggs and Miss Ada passed their days in warmth and comfort and dined on fine food. They ordered beatings and whippings for the farm inhabitants and then slept soundly under feather quilts. They went to church in Sunday finery. They entertained guests. They complained of the detestable poor in their care and the county money wasted upon them.

"Truth to tell," Ira said, "the county's money went to them, not us. They ate beef, and we ate gruel."

A new picture appeared on the TV. Miss Ada sat at a desk, writing in an account book.

"That's the one she showed the county inspector," Caleb told us. "It was all lies."

The camera shifted to Miss Ada's bedroom. She was writing in another account book. When she finished, she put the book in a metal box and locked it.

"That's the true account book," Caleb explained, "for her and Mr. Jaggs, so they'd know how much money they'd hidden away."

"They also wrote the names of those who died and what they died of," Ira added.

"Even the ones they said ran away," Caleb said. "All the names of the dead are in that book."

As he spoke, a new picture formed on the TV screen. Miss Ada was beating Caleb's back with a cane. His shirt was off, and you could count his ribs.

"I'll teach you to steal food!" she yelled as she brought the cane down again and again.

When Caleb's back was bleeding, she thrust him aside and grabbed Ira. "Thief! Liar!" she cried as she beat him.

Last of all, she turned her attention to Seth. "With whom did you share the cheese?" she asked softly. "Tell me, and save yourself a beating."

Seth stared up at the woman, his small face clenched with hatred. "I didn't share it with nobody. I et it all myself."

Miss Ada caressed the cane with her long, slender fingers. "Those children knew the cheese was stolen from my pantry. They must be punished, too."

"I ain't telling you nothing," Seth said.

"Maybe this will change your mind." Miss Ada brought the cane down across his back with a loud *whack*. She paused and looked at him. "Well?"

"You can beat me till you bust your cane," Seth said, wincing from the blow. "I won't tell you nothing."

In horror, Corey and I watched her take the cane to Seth again. When she was through, she called Joseph. "Take these boys outside and leave them there till morning. I want the name of every child who ate that cheese. Perhaps a night in the cold will loosen their lips."

Joseph grabbed the boys as if they were no more than unwanted kittens and dragged them outside. Without a word, he turned and went back into the house. The door slammed. The bolt slid home.

The boys huddled together on the snowy ground, barefoot and coatless. The wind roared in the trees, and icicles shone in the moon's cold light. Slowly, the picture dimmed.

"In the morning, we knew something had changed," Caleb said. "We weren't cold. And we weren't hungry."

"And our backs didn't hurt none from the beating," Seth put in.

"That was almost the strangest part of all," Ira said.

"So we just lay in the snow," Caleb said, "thinking all three of us must be dreaming the same dream."

"Then the back door opened," Ira said, "and Mr. Jaggs

saw us lying on the ground. 'Get up, boys,' he hollered, 'I'm not finished with you!'"

"We rose up to face him," Caleb said, "but our bodies stayed on the ground. That puzzled us greatly."

"We grabbed each other's hands because we felt too light to stay on earth," Ira added. "I reckon that's when we figured out what had happened to us."

Caleb nodded. "The trouble was, we weren't ready to be dead."

Seth sighed. "It weren't fair."

On the screen, Mr. Jaggs strode angrily across the frozen ground toward the boys' huddled bodies. "Get up!" he yelled.

When no one moved, he nudged Seth with his boot. The boy's body rolled over. His sightless eyes stared up at Mr. Jaggs.

The man recoiled. "Dead." He stared at Ira and Seth. "All three."

Frightened, he retreated to the steps and opened the door. "Joseph," he called in a high voice. "Ada. Come quickly."

"What is it?" Miss Ada called from inside. "I've scarcely touched my breakfast."

Joseph appeared in the doorway, looked at the boys, and called to Miss Ada. "Come quickly, Miss."

Holding a dainty teacup, Miss Ada peered over her brother's shoulder. "What's the matter with them?" she asked crossly. "Why don't they get up?"

"Good Lord, Ada, can't you see?" Mr. Jaggs stared at her, his voice shaking. "They're dead."

Miss Ada choked on her tea. "Dead? How can they be dead?"

Joseph stared down at the boys. "It was cold last night, miss, below freezing."

"How do we explain their deaths?" Mr. Jaggs asked.

Miss Ada gripped her teacup, her face pale. "Why, we say what we always say when there's a mishap," she stammered. "They died of fever. Or they ran away."

"But the county inspector is visiting this afternoon," Mr. Jaggs said. "He'll see the bodies. He'll know they froze to death."

Miss Ada seemed to recover her wits. "For heaven's sake, Cornelius. We'll bury them before he arrives and report them as runaways."

"We done similar many times afore," Joseph put in.

"But not on the inspector's visiting day." Mr. Jaggs looked uneasily at the men and women's quarters. "They'll be coming out any moment. They mustn't see the bodies."

The picture dimmed, and a new one slowly formed. Wrapped in sacks, three bodies lay on the ground, screened from the house by a tall, shaggy row of bushes. Near them, Joseph struggled to dig three graves in the cold earth. Neither Mr. Jaggs nor Miss Ada was there to help. The only sound was the thunk of the pickax and the rustle of the wind in the bushes. A bunch of crows streamed past, cawing as they flew. Far away, a dog barked.

Gradually, Corey and I made out the ghostly shapes of the boys standing in the hedge's shadow. They watched Joseph and murmured among themselves.

Every now and then, the man raised his head and looked around, as if he expected to see someone. The boys were invisible to him, but he seemed to sense they were there. He dug faster, cursing to himself, perspiring despite the cold wind.

When the graves were ready, he dumped each boy into the earth and began shoveling dirt on top of their bodies. From a nearby tree, the crows cawed to each other, taking in the scene with their beady eyes.

Joseph shook his fist at the birds and swore loudly. "Get away from here!"

The crows stayed where they were, cawing and hopping from branch to branch as if they were mocking him.

Joseph flattened the earth over the graves. The sound echoed from the barn and the crows cawed louder. When he was done, he marked each grave with a small white stone. As he trudged away, his work done, the camera zoomed in on the stones: 27, 28, and 29. No name, no date—just a number. Slowly, the camera moved back and panned the scene. The stones stood in a row with many others, each marked with a number.

The nameless dead of Fox Hill County Poor Farm lay buried in the very place that had puzzled Corey and me a few days ago.

From the hedge's shadow, the boys crept toward the graves and stared down at them, their faces as sorrowful as mourners at a loved one's burial.

Once more the picture dimmed and faded to black.

13

I ra looked down at us from the top of the bookcase. "Now you know how we came to be what we are," he said.

"The lovely bad ones," Caleb added with a sad smile.

"That's us," Seth boasted.

And the shadow children echoed, "Bad ones, bad ones, lovely bad ones. Lovely, lovely, lovely!"

Caleb wedged himself between Corey and me on the sofa. "We tormented those three from the day we died till the county came snooping around, asking questions they couldn't answer."

"Joseph was the first to skedaddle," Ira said. "We'd just about run him ragged with tricks and pranks. Soon as he heard rumors there'd be an inquiry, he took off."

"Mr. Jaggs was close behind, hugging the money box to his belly." Caleb laughed. "I wish I could've seen his face when he opened it and found nothing inside but old newspapers and stones."

All three laughed. "That were one of our best pranks," Seth said.

"A true gentleman," Ira said. "He left his own sister in the lurch."

Seth sighed. "Then she went and hanged herself and ruined all our fun by becoming a ghost herself."

Ira looked uneasily toward the dark windows. "Better not say more."

"Do you think she heard?" Seth asked in a low voice.

By now, Corey and I were shivering with fear. What we'd seen on the TV screen had been bad enough, but the idea of Miss Ada outside in the dark was even worse. It was all too easy to picture her stalking toward the inn on soundless feet, her face grim, the cane in her hands.

"Can she still hurt you?" Corey whispered.

"Yes, but it's different from before," Caleb said. "In the old days, she beat us and spoke cruelly and starved us and worked us hard."

He hesitated as if he were looking for the right words. When he went on, his voice was so low we had to lean closer to hear him.

"Now all she has to do is *look* at us," he whispered. "There's a darkness in her eyes that brings back all the hurt of being alive. We feel the grief we felt then, the hunger, the thirst, the cold. Every bad thing that happened to us happens over and over. Our folks die. Our little sisters and brothers die. We die."

"And she laughs," Ira hissed in anger.

"When she comes, there's no one to help us," Seth said. "And no place to hide, except in the cold, dark ground."

Neither Corey nor I knew what to say. We just sat there, taking in the awfulness of what we'd heard. The boys watched us. The wind blew harder and the rain pattered like tiny footsteps on the driveway.

"When we go down into the earth," Caleb said at last, "we sleep the way cats do, ready to wake at the least sound."

"If it hadn't been for you," Ira muttered, "we'd be sleeping right now—and so would she."

Seth yawned. "Sometimes it's fun to wake up, but

truth to tell, it wearies me. I wish I could close my eyes and never open them to this world again."

Ira went to the window and peered out. "Watching for her is the worst part. She could be anywhere, you know."

"Not *any*where," Caleb said. "She can't leave this place any more than we can."

Suddenly, the shadow children began to move, flitting this way and that, a child's profile here, the outline of a hand there. Their whispering grew louder. "Run and hide, run and hide."

As Caleb, Seth, and Ira faded into the darkness with the others, a cold wind blew through the window.

"There is no escape for you," a voice cried. "There is no peace!"

The shadow children twisted and turned. They rushed from one corner to another, but they couldn't reach the window or the door. She was already ahead of them, blocking their way out.

Corey leapt to her feet. "Stop," she cried. "Leave them alone!"

A tall shape spun toward us, and we saw Miss Ada's white face, skin stretched tight over her skull, eyes sunk in blackness, hair tangled and coarse. The smell of earth clung to her. She wore the rags of a long dress, but her feet were bare.

"You made a mockery of me," she hissed. "You are as bad as they are. Just wait, you wicked, disrespectful children— you will be punished."

Miss Ada turned back to the shadow children. But they had drifted out the window like smoke, leaving only the echo of laughter behind.

"I'll see to you later!" she shrieked at us and vanished as suddenly as she'd appeared.

Stunned, Corey and I ran to the window, but all we saw was the dark night and the falling rain. Lightning flickered and briefly lit the lawn. The grove crouched silent and still, hiding its secrets.

Long after I went to bed, I lay awake. Miss Ada's face seemed to hang in the dark over me. Her voice rang in my ears.

"I'll see to you later, I'll see to you later, I'll see to you later, later, later, later. . . ."

It was almost light by the time I finally shut off her voice and fell asleep.

Corey hadn't slept any better than I had. We sat at the breakfast table and picked listlessly at our food. Lulled by the monotonous sound of the rain tapping on the windows, we were barely able to keep our eyes open.

Grandmother peered at us. "What's the matter with you two? You look like you didn't sleep a wink last night."

"It's the weather," I mumbled. "This kind of rain makes me feel like staying in bed all day."

Corey yawned so widely I could see her tonsils. "When is it supposed to stop?"

"Sometime this afternoon, the paper says." Grandmother sipped her coffee. "How about a trip to Burlington? We could go shopping to replace the clothes that—" She broke off, her face troubled. "The clothes that were, um, somehow ruined the night those people . . ." Her voice trailed off without finishing the sentence.

It wasn't a night Grandmother liked thinking about. There had been too much she didn't understand, couldn't explain. Too much that didn't fit into her rational view of the world.

Corey and I wasted no time getting ready to go. We needed a break from the inn—and the bad ones—for at least a few hours.

Grandmother had some errands to do on Church Street, so she turned us loose in the Marketplace. "I'll meet you back here in an hour," she said. "We'll have lunch and then shop."

Marketplace was a pedestrian area, kind of like an open-air mall, with plenty of shops, including Gap and a bunch of other big-name stores as well as little-name stores, craft places, and tourist traps. There were fountains and benches and sculptures and lots of open-air eating places deserted because of the rain.

The weather drove us in and out of stores where stuff was too expensive or we already had it or we didn't like it.

We ended up in the Dusty Jacket, a secondhand bookstore, mainly because we'd noticed a huge orange tabby sleeping in the window. Corey wanted to make sure he was real.

"Indeed, he is real." The man behind the counter had a bushy gray beard and thick gray hair. Perched on the end of his nose was a pair of old-fashioned glasses with gold rims. He wore a plaid shirt tucked into faded corduroy trousers. For some reason, I liked him right away.

"A watch cat," he added, "that's what Mog is. He guards the place at night."

Corey poked her head around a display of books to get a better look at Mog. The cat opened one eye a slit, twitched an ear in Corey's direction, and went back to sleep.

"Resting up for his nocturnal rounds," the man said.

"Does he really chase burglars away?" Corey asked.

He laughed. "Well, I've never been burgled, so I reckon he does."

"I bet it's mice he chases," Corey said. "Not burglars."

"Oh, yes, he chases a fair number of mice. Catches them, too. And then lines them up in a row on the counter for me to admire."

While Corey and the man talked, I prowled around the store. Like most used-book stores, there didn't seem to be much order. No Dewey decimal system, for example. Just piles of nice old books with yellowing pages, going soft around the edges.

"Are you looking for anything special?" the man asked.

"Local history, I guess."

"I have lots of local history," he said, "going all the way back to Ethan Allen and the Green Mountain Boys. Ethan was born here, you know. In fact, his brother started the University of Vermont."

He pulled a biography of Ethan Allen off a shelf and showed it to me. "Good read," he said. "I recommend it highly. All yours for fifty cents."

"What we'd really like to find is a history of Fox Hill," Corey said.

"Are you staying at the inn?"

"Our grandmother owns it," I told him.

"Elsie's your grandmother? Well, I'll be. She's one of my regulars, a real nice woman. Comes in sometimes just to visit Mog." He offered his hand. "My name's Jack Pumphrey."

I shook his hand. "I'm Travis Donovan, and this is my sister, Corey."

"What's going on at the inn these days?" Mr. Pumphrey asked. "There were a lot of strange stories before Elsie bought the place, but I haven't heard much lately."

Corey and I exchanged a glance, unsure what to tell Mr. Pumphrey. Taking a deep breath, I decided to ask him what I really wanted to know—*needed* to know. "Do you believe in ghosts?"

Mr. Pumphrey hesitated a moment, as if he, too, wasn't sure what to say. "I hope you won't think I'm crazy for telling you this, but I once saw a ghost myself, right here in this store. Of course, I didn't realize he was a ghost at first. He was standing by that shelf over there, looking at books. There was nothing out of the ordinary about him. But when he left, he walked out through the wall instead of the door. *That* gave me a turn."

Mr. Pumphrey laughed nervously and picked up his cat. "Scared poor Mog, too. He puffed up to twice his normal size and ran and hid. I didn't see him for the rest of the day. He's a real fraidy cat. Thunder and lightning scare him, too."

"Did the ghost ever come back?" Corey asked.

"Not that I know of, but Vera Bartholomew, who runs the antique shop around the corner, claims she's seen the same chap in her place. He's particularly fond of one old armchair. She's thinking it used to belong to him. Could be, I guess, could be."

Mog squirmed, and Mr. Pumphrey set him gently down. "Why are you two so interested in ghosts? Have they showed up at the inn again?"

"Yes, sir," I said. "They sure have."

Deep in thought, brow wrinkled, Mr. Pumphrey stroked his beard. "Ghosts have been seen there off and on for years," he said. "Boys, mostly. And a woman. Hanged herself a long time ago." He reached down to stroke Mog who was rubbing against his legs and purring. "You want your lunch, don't you, sir?"

He straightened up and grinned. "Just last week, some nut driving a hearse came in here with a hippy-dippy woman. They wanted books about Fox Hill, but I didn't have anything that suited them. They both claimed they'd seen ghosts there."

"That was Chester Coakley and Eleanor Duvall," Corey said. "They're psychics. Grandmother accused them of faking the ghosts and threw them out."

Mr. Pumphrey laughed and went on stroking Mog. "That sounds like Elsie. She has her mind closed against any possibility of the supernatural. Won't even discuss it."

"What did you tell them?"

"The truth," he said. "I've always suspected that the previous owners milked the sightings for all they were worth. Maybe even faked them to get publicity for the inn."

"Believe me," I said, "the ghosts at the inn are just as

real as the man you saw walk through the wall of this store."

He gave both of us a long, considering look. "You've actually seen them?"

"Yes, sir," I said.

"Lots of times," Corey put in. "Not just at night, either. We know their names and how they died and what the poor farm was really like."

"And you're not scared?"

"Just of Miss Ada," Corey said. "She's the woman who hanged herself."

"We've made friends with the boys," I said, boasting a little. "They call themselves the bad ones, but they're just ordinary boys."

"Ordinary boys who happen to be dead?" Mr. Pumphrey asked.

"It's not their fault they're dead," Corey said. "Miss Ada left them outside in the cold all night and they froze to death. She's still mean to them—even now when they're all dead, including her, she won't leave them alone."

Mr. Pumphrey looked at us long and hard, as if we'd said something that worried him, maybe even scared him. "Let me give you some advice," he said. "Stay away from those boys. The dead have their place. And the living have theirs. It's dangerous to cross the line that separates them from us."

For a moment, he watched the raindrops race one another down the shop's window, thinking of what to say next. "It's one thing to watch a ghost walk through a wall," he said slowly. "It's something else to ask him how he did it."

"We couldn't stay away from those boys even if we wanted to," I told Mr. Pumphrey. "They follow us everywhere."

Just then the bell over the door jangled, and a rosy-faced woman rushed inside, struggling to close her umbrella. "Has the book I ordered come in?" she asked Mr. Pumphrey.

"Excuse me, children." He turned to the woman. "I was just about to call you, Abigail. *The Murder at the Vicarage* arrived in this morning's mail. It's in good condition—a little foxing, but on the whole it's a fine first edition."

As Mr. Pumphrey handed the book to Abigail, Corey nudged me. "It's past twelve. Grandmother's going to be mad if we keep her waiting much longer."

"We have to go," I told Mr. Pumphrey. "We're supposed to meet our grandmother."

Abigail handed her credit card to Mr. Pumphrey. "Thanks so much for getting this for me. It's the only Agatha Christie first edition I don't have."

As he ran the card through his machine, Mr. Pumphrey watched us open the door. "Say hello to Elsie for me," he said. "And remember, you can't trust the dead. They go by different rules than the living."

Mog meowed as if he, too, wished to warn us. Then he hopped into the window and watched us run toward Church Street.

Huddled under her umbrella, Grandmother frowned when she saw us. "I've been waiting for fifteen minutes. Where have you been?"

"At the Dusty Jacket." I pointed down the brick walkway to the little building squeezed between the Nearly New Emporium and the Vermont Crafts Shop. "Mr. Pumphrey said to say hello for him."

Grandmother's frown turned to a smile. "Jack Pumphrey can talk the ear off a rabbit. Did you meet his cat?"

"Mog's huge," Corey said, "and so sweet and pretty. I wish I had a cat just like him."

"He's also a great mouse killer," I said.

"So I've heard." Grandmother started walking down Church Street, dodging puddles and other people's umbrellas. "What would you like to eat?"

"Pizza," Corey and I said. It was the one thing Mrs. Brewster never fixed and probably never would.

"I know just the place," Grandmother said.

The windows of Nel's Pizzeria were steamed up, giving it a cozy, welcoming look. As soon as we stepped inside, we smelled tomato sauce and cheese and baking pie crust. Crowds of college kids occupied most of the tables, but the service was quick, and we soon had a pizza the size of the moon, gooey with cheese, runny with tomato sauce, and topped with meatballs the size of a baby's fist.

"How does it compare with New York pizza?" Grandmother asked.

When Corey and I both gave thumbs up, she looked at our empty plates and laughed. "Foolish me. I thought we'd have enough left over for an after-dinner snack."

Stuffed with pizza, we headed for Wade's of Vermont, where Grandmother bought us each a pair of jeans, two pairs of shorts, three T-shirts, and extra underwear and socks.

"Let's hope nothing happens to these," she said. "I can't afford to replace them."

"Don't worry. The ghosts like us now," Corey said. "Except for Miss Ada, of course. She hates—"

Grandmother stopped right in the middle of the sidewalk and stared at Corey. Rain dripped off her umbrella and splashed into the puddles. "What are you talking about?"

Corey's face turned red with embarrassment. "Just because you don't believe in ghosts doesn't mean they aren't real."

"Not that ghost nonsense again," Grandmother said. "Sensible people simply do not subscribe to such foolishness."

"How about Mr. Pumphrey?" I asked. "Do you think he's sensible?"

"Jack's a bit eccentric, but I suppose he's fairly sensible." She looked at me closely. "Are you saying Jack Pumphrey believes in ghosts?"

"He's seen one in his shop," Corey said. "And so has the lady who runs the antique store."

"And so have *you*," I said. "You just won't admit it."

By now Grandmother was unlocking the truck. "Get in out of the rain," she said crossly. As she edged out of her parking space, she said, "Not another word about ghosts!"

Corey and I looked at each other. We'd have something to say to each other when we got home, but for now we'd keep our mouths shut.

14

After we'd put our new clothes away, Corey and I went outside for a walk. The rain had stopped, but the lawn was puddled with water. Our shoes were soon soaked, but we slogged through the mud, not paying much attention to where we were going.

"Is Mr. Pumphrey right about the boys?" Corey asked. "Are they dangerous?"

"No matter what he says, I'm not scared of them," I said. "They're just kids."

"*Dead* kids," Corey reminded me.

"Save your worries for Miss Ada. *She's* the dangerous one."

Corey gnawed on a fingernail, her face worried. "What do you think they want?"

"Maybe we should ask them."

As luck would have it, I'd no sooner spoken than I realized we'd wandered into the burial ground. Caleb, Seth, and Ira grinned down at us from an apple tree. The shadow children clustered around them, a profile here, a leg dangling there, a hand holding a limb—like one of those pictures where you have to find hidden objects.

"We been waiting on you," Seth called.

Jumping down from the tree, the bad ones led us to a row of stones.

"This here's mine," Seth said. "And there's Caleb's and

Ira's. But who's to know withouten our names writ on 'em?"

Corey looked at him solemnly. "Travis and I can write your names on these three stones."

"That's right kindly of you," Seth said, "but we want proper headstones, like you see in a church graveyard."

"And not just for us," Caleb said. "For *all* the folks lying here forgotten."

"Do you know their names?"

"Course not," Seth said. "None of us ever seen a burial."

"Joseph dug the graves at night," Ira explained. "By sunup, the job was done, and we didn't know who was put where."

"Until we became as we are now," Caleb corrected him. "We mourned all the folk they buried here after us. Said the right words for them and tried to send them over the river to the place where they belonged."

The shadows stirred. "We stayed, though," they whispered. "All us boys, all us bad ones—we stayed."

"There's just one here with a name." Seth pushed his way through a thick tangle of bushes and honeysuckle vines and pointed. "There she lies."

A cracked stone lay face-up on the ground, covered with so much moss I had to scrape it off before I could read the inscription:

MISS ADA JAGGS
3 APRIL 1789 – 17 MARCH 1841
A WICKED HEART IS ITS OWN REWARD

Corey pressed against my side. "A wicked heart," she whispered.

"It's true, ain't it?" Seth asked.

"Her heart was wicked through and through and black with hate," Ira said quietly.

"Who wrote the inscription?" I asked.

"A man from the county office ordered it done," Caleb said. "But it was our idea. We whispered it to him so sweetly he thought it was *his* idea."

Ira kicked Miss Ada's stone. "He wanted to put names on all our markers, but he couldn't find the burial records."

"That's 'cause he didn't know about her secret account book," Seth said.

"Now if you two were to find *that*," Caleb added, "everybody could have their proper stones. And maybe we could rest easy."

"Are you saying Corey and I . . . have to find Miss Ada's book?" I stared at Caleb. "Don't *you* know where it is?"

"She used to keep it under the floor in her room," Caleb said.

"But she could have hidden it somewhere else," Ira pointed out.

"After all, we wasn't watching her every second of every day, was we?" Seth asked.

"Do you remember which room was hers?" I asked Caleb.

"Number seven." He pointed at a window on the second floor, the Jenningses' old room, the one with a good view of the grove . . . and the stupid ghost imitation that had started all the trouble.

Corey looked at me. "Is anyone staying there?"

"I think it's those two old ladies, Miss Baynes and Miss Edwards," I said.

Seth giggled. "I sure riled them up with that mouse at dinner, didn't I?"

"I *thought* that was you," Corey said, laughing herself.

"They're usually gone all day," I said, in an effort to steer everyone's attention back to the room—and to the account book that might or might not be hidden there.

"Let's see if we can find it." Corey ran to the inn with me close behind. The bad ones followed us on soundless feet, blending in with the shadow children.

We paused at the front door and listened. All was silent except for the grandfather clock ticking to itself in the hall. While Corey kept watch, I sneaked into the office and lifted the spare key to room 7 from its hook.

On tiptoe, we crept up the wide stairs to the second floor and paused again to listen. The doors to the occupied rooms were closed. The other doors were open. We didn't hear Mrs. Brewster's vacuum cleaner, nor did we see any other signs that she was cleaning the rooms.

Cautiously, we approached number 7. I knocked, but there was no answer.

"Nobody's home," Seth said.

Slowly, I stuck the key in the lock and turned it gently. Feeling like a burglar, I eased the door open. Corey and I— and the bad ones—stepped inside. I locked the door behind us. The room was empty. A pink sweater hung on the back of a chair, and a pair of neatly folded tan slacks lay on the seat. Shopping bags from Simon Pearce sat in the corner. On the desk was an assortment of tin cookie cutters made by Ann Clark of Vermont. Grandmother had dozens of them, and so did our mother. Not that Mom ever baked—she collected them and displayed them on a wall in the kitchen.

But we hadn't come to look at cookie cutters. On our hands and knees, we crawled across the floor looking for loose boards. We covered every inch, but each board was nailed down tightly.

"Maybe we should pull them up," Ira suggested.

"No," I said as Seth tugged at a board. "Try the walls. Maybe there's a hole behind something."

We started with the little Currier and Ives prints and moved on to the mirrors. As Corey and I struggled to move a tall pine bureau, Seth said, "*Hsst*—the old ladies are back!"

Just as he spoke, I heard Miss Baynes say to Miss Edwards, "Shopping tires me out more than it used to. Let's have a rest before dinner."

They were in the hall, right outside the door. As one of them put a key in the lock, Corey and I slid under one of the beds. Hidden by a floor-length dust ruffle, we heard the women enter the room, accompanied by the rustle of more shopping bags.

"Woodstock was just delightful," Miss Edwards said. "So many nice stores."

"And lunch was delicious," Miss Baynes said. "If the inn at Woodstock wasn't so expensive, I'd cancel our reservations here and take a room there."

"I'm sure we wouldn't see a mouse in the dining room."

"Indeed not."

The bathroom door opened and shut behind Miss Edwards, and Miss Baynes lay down on her bed. The mattress creaked and sagged over our heads. Corey and I scarcely dared to breathe.

Suddenly, Miss Baynes sneezed and sat up with a jerk.

The bathroom door opened, and Miss Edwards said, "What's the matter?"

"Someone just tickled my nose with a feather!"

Miss Edwards laughed. "You must have been dreaming." The next second her laugh turned into a gasp. "My sweater!" she cried. "It just floated out the window!"

Both women ran to look. "There it is!" Miss Baynes said. "It's caught on the branch of a tree. See? The wind must have blown it there."

"But it's not windy," Miss Edwards said.

That's when the giggling started.

"What's that?" Miss Baynes asked.

Little ripples of laughter ran around the walls.

"It sounds as if someone is having a joke at our expense." Miss Edwards opened the closet door. "Come out, right now!"

The giggles got louder. At the same moment, a Simon Pearce shopping bag slid across the floor and bumped against Miss Edwards's legs. A few small pictures fell off the wall, and the bathroom door opened and shut three times.

As the women ran from the room, Seth joined us under the bed. Convulsed with laughter, he drummed his heels on the floor. "That was fun," he crowed.

Corey gave him an annoyed look. "They'll leave for sure now."

Following her lead, I slid out from under the bed and left the room while we had the opportunity. Seth came with us, hiccupping from laughing so much.

Behind the office's closed door, Miss Baynes and Miss Edwards were complaining to Grandmother. "It must be your grandchildren," Miss Edwards said.

"Didn't they cause enough disturbance in the dining room with their childish pranks?" Miss Baynes asked.

We didn't wait to hear Grandmother's answer. Sneaking out to the porch, we sat down in the rocking chairs farthest from the front door.

Seth joined us and rocked happily back and forth, his red curls blowing in the breeze he generated.

Corey glared at him. "We get blamed for everything you do. It's not fair!"

Seth scowled. "You think dying when you're just seven's fair?"

"Nothing's fair," I said. "You're both old enough to know that."

"Not me," Seth said. "I weren't old enough when I died to know about what's fair and what's not."

"Well, you're a lot older than seven now," Corey said.

"No, I ain't. I was seven then and I'm seven now and I'll always be seven. So there."

"What if you had to be ninety-nine forever?" Corey asked. "And you had to hobble around and you couldn't see or hear and—"

I gave her a nudge with my elbow. "Shut up, Corey. You're giving me a headache."

"I was just trying to say—"

"Well, stop trying," I said. "Seth isn't even here anymore."

She looked around, surprised. While we'd been arguing, Seth had disappeared.

A little later, Miss Edwards and Miss Baynes stalked out of the inn. Mr. Brewster followed them, hauling their little wheeled suitcases and all their shopping bags. We sat very still and hoped they wouldn't see us.

Without looking to the right or the left, they got into their Honda and slammed the doors. As soon as Mr. Brewster had wedged everything into the trunk, they took off, driving faster than the average person their age, I thought.

"All that," I said, "and we didn't even find the account book."

15

I've been thinking." Ira appeared on the porch railing, looking glum, as usual. "Maybe she buried the book in the grove before she hanged herself."

I imagined Corey and me digging one hole after another, fighting roots and rocks with our shovels, sweating in the heat, bitten by gnats and mosquitoes—not a pretty picture.

"What makes you think so?" Corey asked.

"Well, she wouldn't leave it in her room, would she? Somebody might find it there." He pushed his dark hair out of his eyes. "Most likely she reckoned nobody would dig up the grove."

"Why would they?" Caleb sat down next to Ira, swinging his bare feet. "Nobody knew there *was* another book."

"But it's spooky in the grove." Corey toyed with her fingers, twisting them this way and that, as if she wanted to tie them into a knot.

"Spooooky," Seth whispered in her ear, "*Spooooky*."

"Go away." Corey swatted at him as if he were an annoying fly. "You get on my nerves."

Seth pulled the barrettes out of Corey's hair and laughed as long strands fell in her face.

Corey got up so fast the rocker swung wildly back and forth. "Quit it!" she yelled at Seth.

Grandmother heard the noise and came to the door.

"I've been looking for you two," she said. Her voice was calm but stern, and she had a teacherly gleam in her eye that meant Trouble, with a capital T. "Come inside. I want to talk to you."

Seth giggled and made a face. "Nyah, nyah, you're in for it now!"

Ira grabbed the younger boy's arm. "Leave off."

The three faded from sight, and Corey and I followed Grandmother into the office.

"I'm very disappointed in your behavior," she began. "Because of your pranks, Miss Baynes and Miss Edwards have canceled the rest of their stay here. They—"

"We didn't do anything to them," I said.

"It was Seth," Corey added. "We told him not to, but—"

"Seth?" Grandmother stared at Corey. "Please don't tell me he's one of your ghosts."

"But he is," Corey insisted. "He's the worst one of all, he's—"

"Corey, I simply can't believe this." Grandmother turned to me. "Travis, tell me the truth. Why did you let a mouse loose in the dining room last night? And why did you booby-trap room seven? What on earth do you have against those two women?"

"Corey's not lying," I said. "It *was* Seth."

"Seth." Grandmother drummed her fingers on her desk top. "Seth."

"Yes'm?" Seth came as if in answer to his name. "What is it you want?" He drummed on the desk, too.

Grandmother jerked her hands back, but the drumming went on. She looked right through Seth at Corey and me. We held up our hands to show we weren't—couldn't be—responsible. Thanks to the shadow children, the sound had gotten much louder.

"Stop making that noise!" Grandmother raised her voice to be heard above the drumming. She was plainly frightened but trying hard not to be.

"It's not us," I said.

"It's Seth," Corey said, "and the others."

"I'm going to call your parents right now and tell them to come and get you," Grandmother shouted. "I cannot allow you to destroy the inn's reputation. Not to mention my sanity!"

As she reached for the phone, Seth picked up an eraser and threw it across the room, followed by a handful of pens and pencils. A stapler rose into the air and floated a few inches from Grandmother's nose. The printer churned out a stream of blank paper, the computer flickered on and off, and the radio suddenly changed from classical music to loud rock. Doors and windows opened and shut with loud bangs, and a swivel chair spun as it rolled around the room, banging into walls.

Grandmother just sat there, watching the office dim and brighten as the shadow children filled the air with a blizzard of spinning paperclips and thumbtacks.

"It's true," she whispered. "The inn really is haunted . . . everything I've believed is wrong." With that she put her head down on her folded arms and closed her eyes.

"Now look what you've done!" Corey yelled. "You've upset Grandmother!"

The shadow children giggled and retreated, but Seth

plopped down on the edge of Grandmother's desk. Regarding her sadly, he touched her hair.

Grandmother shuddered and looked up. "You must be Seth." Her voice was weak, but she seemed to be back in control.

"You can see me now." He looked pleased.

"Yes."

"That's 'cause you believe in me." He grinned. "Sorry I had to scare you into it, but you was a hard nut to crack."

Ira and Caleb appeared on either side of Seth. "Sorry, ma'am," Caleb said. "But we couldn't let you send Corey and Travis away."

"We need them to help us, you see," Ira added.

"Even though they're none too smart," Seth put in. "But we ain't found nobody else. Most folks just run off, like them silly old ladies."

"Or they try to trap us with machines of one sort or another," Ira said. "Cameras and the like."

"Those psychos got no business messing with us," Seth said. "If we wanted our pictures took, we'd pose."

"Psychics," Caleb corrected him. "That's what they call themselves nowadays."

Grandmother just sat there staring at the boys as if she was too stunned to say a word. Finally, she said, "What do you want my grandchildren to do?

"Just three things," Caleb told her.

"Truth to tell," Seth piped up, "they's a hard three things."

"First, they have to find Miss Ada's secret account book," Caleb went on, "the one that has the names of the dead who are buried here."

"Then they have to mark the graves with proper stones," Ira said, "the kind with names, not numbers, wrote on them."

"And last, they got to exercise Miss Ada," Seth said.

"Exorcise," Corey said.

Seth frowned. "That's what I said."

"No, you didn't," Corey said. "You—"

I gave her a little sideways kick. "Drop it."

"Yes," Seth said. "Drop it or I'll drop you."

"Stop squabbling," Grandmother said as if she were in her fourth-grade classroom. With a sigh, she leaned back in her chair. She looked very tired. "I don't understand any of this," she said.

"We'll explain it to you," I said.

Grandmother closed her eyes. "I'm listening."

Helped here and there by the bad ones, Corey and I told Grandmother everything we knew about the poor farm; Miss Ada Jaggs and her brother, Cornelius; the burial ground; the secret account book; and so on. By the time we were done, it was almost five o'clock.

Wearily, Grandmother got to her feet. "I don't know what to think," she murmured. "I just don't know."

Mrs. Brewster chose that moment to appear in the doorway. "Time for dinner," she said, and then gasped when she noticed the mess the bad ones had made. "It's them again, ain't it?"

Without hesitating, she plunged her hand into a particularly dark corner and hauled Seth out by his shirt front. "Naughty boy," she said. "Why can't you stay where you belong and stop causing trouble?"

Seth squirmed and wiggled, but he couldn't break away

from her. "Let me go, Aunt Martha!" he yelled. "I don't need you looking after me. I can take care of my own self!"

While we stared at her, Mrs. Brewster shrugged. "You might say me and Henry inherited this here boy. He's my great-great-great-grandfather's nephew. The care of him's been passed down from generation to generation. We try to protect him, like his mama wished, but he sleeps light. Don't take much to wake him up."

Without releasing the struggling Seth, she gave Corey and me a dark look. "You and your thoughtless ghost games," she muttered. "This here boy is suffering on account of you. Why didn't you leave him be?"

"Don't go blaming them," Seth said. "They didn't know no better."

"*You* know who's to blame, Mrs. Brewster," Caleb said. "But you're scared to face her."

With a final jerk, Seth pulled away from Mrs. Brewster. Shielding himself with Caleb, he stuck out his tongue. "I don't need no aunties looking after me."

Then they were gone.

"So you knew all about this, Martha?" Grandmother asked.

"Small chance you'd have believed me even if I'd told you."

"Too true." Grandmother sighed. "I used to believe the dead rested in peace. After my husband died, it was a consolation of sorts." She turned her head and looked out the window. 'Fear no more the heat o' the sun,'" she murmured, "'Nor the furious winter's rages.'"

The bad ones had quoted the same lines. Like them, like

Corey and me, Grandmother was learning there might be plenty to fear after death.

"Most do rest in peace," Mrs. Brewster said softly. "Live a good life and die a good death—that's all you got to do. Those two things." She rubbed her hands together and added, "I came to tell you dinner is served."

With that, she strode out of the office.

"'Live a good life and die a good death,'" Grandmother said. "If only it were that simple."

After we'd finished eating the best steak I'd ever sunk my teeth into, the inn's only guests stopped at our table.

"Did Miss Baynes and Miss Edwards leave early?" Mrs. Kowalski asked. "We'd planned an afternoon at Lake Bomoseen tomorrow."

"Unfortunately, they had . . . a change of plans," Grandmother said.

"It would have been nice if they'd told us." Mrs. Kowalski patted her frosted hair, showing off her perfectly polished nails. "George and I were looking forward to getting to know them better. Such dears."

Grandmother regarded the woman over the rim of her coffee cup. "They left in a hurry."

"Oh, dear." Mrs. Kowalski pressed a stray strand of hair more firmly into place. "It wasn't an emergency, was it?"

"I don't think so." Grandmother set her cup in its saucer. *Clink.*

Mrs. Kowalski lingered a moment. When it became clear that Grandmother wasn't going to tell her anything else, she said, "I guess George and I will drive to Bomoseen without them."

With her husband trailing behind, like a dog trained to heel, Mrs. Kowalski headed for the porch and the rocking chairs.

Grandmother looked at Corey and me. "I can't believe I'm saying this," she said with a sigh, "but something must be done about the ghosts. We're completely booked next week. I can't afford to lose my guests."

Mrs. Brewster appeared at Grandmother's elbow. "More coffee?"

"Yes, please," Grandmother said. "And do join us, Martha. I need all the help I can get with this ghost business."

Almost on cue, the light dimmed slightly as the shadow children filled the corners. Caleb, Ira, and Seth pulled extra chairs over and sat down, their faces hopeful.

"I wish I could have some of that there coffee." Seth sniffed so deeply his nose wrinkled. "It sure smells good."

"Coffee's not for boys," Grandmother said. "When you grow up, you can drink all you want."

"Grow up?" Seth stared at Grandmother. "When do you think I'll do that, Granny?"

Grandmother actually blushed. "I'm sorry," she said, "I wasn't thinking." She poured a cup from Mrs. Brewster's pot and held it toward him.

Seth didn't take it. "I reckon you forgot I'm dead and I can't drink nothing. Nor can I eat."

"Oh, dear." Grandmother's face turned even redder.

Seth touched her hand. "It's all right, Granny. It's plain you ain't used to dining with the likes of us."

Mrs. Brewster leaned toward Seth. "We've got impor-
tant matters to discuss, so sit still and be quiet or I'll call
Henry. He'll fix your wagon."

"Uncle Henry can't do nothing to me." But Seth sat
back in his chair and folded his hands in his lap, the very
model of a good boy.

Grandmother turned to Martha. "The boys here say
they want three things done: First, Miss Ada's account
book must be found. It contains the names of the people
buried here. With it, we can match the numbers on the
grave markers with the names of the dead."

Mrs. Brewster nodded. "She kept two books, but the one
you want, the true one, was never found. Me and Henry
have looked, and so have all our kin before us."

"We'll find it." Grandmother looked at Corey and me as
if she expected us to solve the problem by pulling the book
out of thin air.

"Secondly," she went on, "we must erect proper headstones for the graves."

"It would comfort the poor souls," Mrs. Brewster said
with another nod, "to know they've not been forgot."

"And thirdly . . . " Grandmother hesitated as if she
dreaded saying the last one. "Thirdly, Miss Ada must be
exorcised."

Mr. Brewster spoke up from the doorway. "She won't go
willingly. Not that one."

The shadow children twittered like scared baby birds,
and all three bad ones folded their arms tightly across their
chests and looked grim.

"She's got to go," Caleb said. "Or there'll be no peace
for us—or you, either."

"What can we do?" Grandmother asked.

"*You* can't do anything," Ira said in his deepest and most serious voice. "The ones who started this must be the ones who finish it."

Corey grabbed my hand and stared at the bad ones. "Do you mean us?"

"Granny wasn't the one flitting around the grove in her nightie," Seth said. "Nor was Aunt Martha."

"If I recollect rightly," Caleb put in, "it was you, Corey—with Travis helping."

Grandmother frowned at us. "I always suspected it was you two."

"Me and Henry knew all along," Mrs. Brewster said. "They're a pair of bad ones themselves, full of sass and mischief just like Seth here."

I bit my lip to keep from grinning. There was no denying it. We *were* bad ones, always in trouble—but not wicked. Like to like, the lovely bad ones—Corey and me and Seth, Caleb, and Ira. I glanced at Corey but failed to catch her eye. She sat beside Grandmother playing with a strand of her hair, thinking her own thoughts.

"Even if this is Corey and Travis's fault," Grandmother said, "I can't allow them to endanger themselves. Good or bad or just plain mischievous, they're my grandchildren. I'm responsible for their well-being—and I love them."

"I agree with Caleb," Mr. Brewster said. "Your grandchildren got us into this mess. It's only fair they get us out of it."

"After all," Mrs. Brewster put in, "Miss Ada can't kill them or hurt them. The worst she can do is scare them."

"But how can we get rid of her?" Corey whispered.

And how do you know she can't hurt us, I wondered.

"After the first two things are done," Caleb said, "we'll come up with a way to send Miss Ada wherever she must go next."

I hoped Caleb was right, but for now I didn't want to think about facing Miss Ada. Not with darkness coming on.

16

The night passed quietly. No visits from the bad ones. No visits from Miss Ada. I slept dreamlessly and woke to a morning full of sunshine and bird song. Not that I expected it to stay that way for long. Miss Ada was sure to cause problems before the day was over.

As soon as we'd eaten breakfast, Corey and I borrowed a couple of shovels from Mr. Brewster (without telling him, because we didn't want him asking questions) and went in search of the bad ones. We found them exactly where we'd expected them to be, stretched out on tree limbs in the grove, waiting for us.

Seth dropped down from a limb at least three stories above the ground. Ira and Caleb landed on either side of him like apples falling from a tree.

"Where should we start digging?" I asked.

"That's where she hanged herself." Seth pointed to a twisted tree that cast an especially dark shadow. "And this here's the very branch." Like a monkey, he jumped up and grabbed a long limb. Swinging back and forth, he said, "She turned and she twisted and she—"

"Hush!" Ira grabbed Seth and pulled him back to earth. "What do you think you're doing?"

As he spoke, Miss Ada's tree shook, as if a gust of wind were blowing through it. Its leaves rustled, and its branches creaked. A dozen or so crows shot out of their roosting places and flew away, almost deafening us with their loud cries.

At the same moment, the shade under the tree deepened and darkened, and the temperature dropped so low I shivered. On the ground, a shadow swung back and forth, as if cast by a body hanging from a rope.

Suddenly, Miss Ada was there, twisting on her rope, her distorted face a hideous shade of purple. "You won't find it," she said with an evil smile. "It's hidden where no one dares look."

The bad ones began to sob and tremble and cry out, as if remembering beatings and hunger and cold winter winds, the deaths of loved ones, things lost and gone forever, babies' cries and mothers' prayers.

Terrified of Miss Ada's power, Corey and I dropped our shovels and grabbed the bad ones' hands. Pulling them along with us, we fled from the cold grove. Our ears rang with their cries, our eyes burned with their tears. Like them, we felt again every pain and loss we'd ever suffered.

On the sunlit lawn, we fell to earth in a heap, aching with misery and shaking with fear.

"See what you did?" Caleb yelled at Seth, who was still crying for his mother. "You woke Miss Ada with your foolish shenanigans!"

"Didn't I warn you?" Ira cried. "Didn't I tell you—"

"I'm sorry." Seth kept on weeping. "I forgot, I was just funning, I didn't mean—"

"Oh, stop your crying," Caleb said more gently. "I shouldn't have shouted at you. When she brings the old pains back, they hurt so bad I can't hardly think straight."

Seth wiped his eyes with his dirty fists. "I want my mama, I want my pa. I hate this place."

"All of us hate being here," Caleb murmured.

"We were unlucky," Ira said. "You and Caleb and me and everyone else who ever lived and died on this poor farm."

While the bad ones talked among themselves, I stole a quick look at the grove. In my mind's eye, I saw Miss Ada hanging from the tree, her feet dancing in the air, her face contorted. My stomach heaved, and I thought I was going to throw up.

But there was no sign of her now. One by one, the crows flew back and settled themselves noisily in the trees.

With a shudder, I touched Caleb's shoulder. "What did Miss Ada mean when she said the book was hidden where no one would dare to look?"

He frowned, his forehead as wrinkled as an old man's. "Maybe it's buried with her."

"That's impossible," Corey said. "Dead people can't take things with them."

"Mr. Jaggs could have put it there," Ira said.

"But he ran away," I said.

Ira nodded. "But he sneaked back after Miss Ada hanged herself."

"She was laid out in the parlor," Caleb explained, "the guest lounge you call it now. He came to see her in the dead of night."

Ira looked up from the clover chain he was making. "We were scared to go near the house with her lying there, but we saw the old codger steal away before day-break. He had plenty of time to leave the book with her."

Pausing to knot another clover stem, he added, "As she said, who'd dare look for it there?"

"Not me!" Corey glanced across the sunny lawn at the grove and shuddered. At the same time, I shook my head.

The bad ones fixed us with their mournful stares. "You promised," Caleb reminded us.

Ira nodded, his dark eyes solemn. "It's the first thing, remember?"

"Find the names and make the proper gravestones," Seth said in case we'd forgotten.

"No one can rest in peace if you don't," Caleb added.

"Even if the book *is* there," Corey put in, "it's rotted away by now."

"Not if it's in the metal box where she always kept it," Caleb pointed out.

I shook my head again. "No way. Impossible. Forget it. I'm not doing it." Expecting Corey to follow me, I jumped up and started to walk away, but when I looked back, she was still sitting on the grass with the bad ones.

"Where are you going?" she called.

I stopped, unsure what to do. I was ashamed to admit it, but part of me (a *big* part) wanted to call Mom and Dad and tell them I was coming home. I'd hitchhike if I had to. Anything to get away from this place.

Trailed by the bad ones, Corey ran to my side. "Don't you dare walk out now, Travis. We *promised* to help them."

"But we can't dig up—"

"You big yellow belly," Seth said. "Don't you go and skedaddle."

"Listen here," Caleb put in. "She's not in her grave anyway. She's over yonder." He pointed at the grove.

"She doesn't always stay there," I reminded him.

He didn't have an answer for that.

"She's naught but rags and bones if that's what scaring you," Seth said.

Frankly, that was plenty scary.

"We have to find the book," Corey said. "We *have* to. No matter what happens."

Seth turned to me with a sneer. "Ain't you ashamed to be bested by a girl? You're nothing but a sissified nancy boy."

"Don't call him names," Ira told Seth. "You'll just make him mad. And what good will that do?"

Seth scowled at me. "Nancy boy," he muttered again. "Where's your dress? And your hair ribbons?"

"Be quiet, Seth," Caleb said.

"I'll say what I like." As he spoke, Seth put some distance between himself and Caleb.

While Caleb's attention was focused on Seth, Corey took me aside. "I'm scared, too," she whispered. "In fact, I'm terrified, but we don't have any choice—and you know it."

What could I say? She was right. Since my legs were shaking too hard to stand up, I sank down on the grass near Caleb. "Okay, okay," I croaked, "we'll do it."

Caleb sighed with relief. "Meet us at her grave tonight."

"Why not do it now," I asked, "while the sun's shining?"

"Nobody digs up graves in broad daylight," Ira said.

"It's got to be done proper," Seth added, still keeping his distance from Caleb.

"At the stroke of twelve," Caleb said. "The time it's been told in stories since way past when."

With that, the bad ones pulled one of their vanishing acts, and Corey and I found ourselves alone on the lawn.

"Midnight," I muttered. "They're making it as hard as they can."

I glanced at my watch. We had almost twelve hours to kill before we tried our luck at grave robbing.

17

Fortunately for us, Grandmother was too busy dealing with a surprise vanload of senior citizens to pay much attention to Corey and me. Mrs. Brewster had made an emergency trip to Middlebury to buy food for the unexpected guests, and Mr. Brewster was occupied schlepping suitcases and other paraphernalia.

Taking advantage of the activity, Corey and I lay low at the swimming pool all afternoon. If no one saw us, we wouldn't have to answer any questions.

When we showed up for dinner, the dining room was packed with laughing people, talking loudly and roaming from table to table taking pictures of each other. No one saw Seth poking his head into every group shot, showing off his gap-toothed grin.

Caleb and Ira contented themselves with watching from the ceiling fan. Round and round they went, their faces solemn, causing no disturbance, for once.

Mrs. Brewster lingered at our table. "The bad ones are here. Did you notice?"

"Yes." Grandmother watched Seth strike a silly pose for a lady with a video camera. "Will he show up when she looks at her pictures?"

"She'll think the camera's broke," Mrs. Brewster answered. "All her pictures will be ruined by white streaks—like light got in."

When Mrs. Brewster crossed the room to refill water glasses, Grandmother turned to us. "Have you made any progress finding the account book?"

We shook our heads and busied ourselves with the chicken Parmesan, another excellent gourmet treat from Mrs. Brewster.

"Even though I can see those boys, I still find it hard to believe my own eyes." Grandmother frowned at the perfect green bean she'd speared. "Was it a mistake to send those psychics away?"

Ira dropped down from the fan and took a seat beside her. "They were flimflammers," he said. "You were right to tell them to leave."

Seth took a seat on her other side. "No matter what they tell you, folks can't catch us with those fancy ghost-hunting machines."

"What about priests?" Grandmother asked. "Does exorcism work?"

"Rarely," Ira said. "The trouble is they usually don't take the time to get to know spirits. If you don't know what's holding us here, you can't make us leave."

Grandmother started to laugh. "I'm sorry," she told the bad ones who looked not only puzzled but hurt by her giggles. "I just can't believe I'm actually having this conversation. Sometimes I'm convinced I've lost my mind and I'm hallucinating."

The bad ones looked at each other as if they were both thinking the same thing. "Maybe you are," Ira said in that solemn way of his, ". . . hallucinating."

Grandmother smiled. "Actually, I wouldn't mind if I were temporarily insane. At least I'd have a chance of regaining my faith in a rational world where the dead stay dead and don't swing on chandeliers." While she spoke, she watched Seth perform acrobatic feats overhead.

One of the new guests pointed at the chandelier. "Look at that!"

"What's making it swing?" another asked.

As the diners sat staring, their chicken forgotten, Seth imitated the daring young man on the flying trapeze. He was, of course, invisible to them.

An elderly woman gasped and got to her feet. "It's going to fall!" she cried.

As the guests began to hurry out of the room, Caleb and Ira joined Seth and told him to stop. With Seth protesting loudly, all three vanished, and the chandelier slowly came to a stop.

Grandmother hastened after the guests. "It's all right," she assured them. "The chandelier does that sometimes. It's stopped now. Please come back and have dessert. Martha's prepared a double chocolate cake with her own special raspberry sauce. It's absolutely delicious."

Murmuring to themselves, the guests returned reluctantly to their tables. Mrs. Brewster hustled about, serving generous slices of dark chocolate cake sitting in pools of raspberry sauce.

Although the guests eyed the chandelier from time to time, the cake placated them. Soon the room filled again with voices and laughter.

Grandmother looked at the people at the other tables and sighed. "Just think," she said slowly, "once I was as ignorant as they are."

Corey and I went on eating, savoring each bite of cake

as if it might be our last. Grandmother sipped her coffee, her cake untouched.

Mrs. Brewster passed our table on her way to offer more coffee to the guests. "Isn't it to your liking?" she asked Grandmother.

"The cake?" Grandmother touched it with her fork. "Sorry, Martha. I'm sure it's delicious, but I'm not very hungry tonight."

"Nothing affects the children's appetites," Mrs. Brewster observed.

"Are you offering seconds?" I asked.

"It's all gone." With that, Mrs. Brewster bustled across the room to refill coffee cups.

"Bummer," I muttered.

"Here, split mine between you." Grandmother slid her plate toward us.

"Are you sure you don't want it?" Corey asked.

Grandmother nodded. "Take it, please. We don't want to hurt Martha's feelings."

Grandmother watched us eat and then excused herself to sit on the porch for a while. By the time we joined her, she was surrounded by the guests. One woman had read *Haunted Inns* and was full of questions.

"Have you seen any ghosts?" she asked. "Heard any strange sounds? Felt cold spots?"

Grandmother shook her head, but she didn't meet the woman's eyes.

"When that chandelier started to swing, I thought it was ghosts, for sure," the woman said with a nervous laugh.

The other guests chuckled uneasily. "That's the strangest thing I've ever seen," one said.

"You say it happens often?" another asked.

Grandmother pressed her hand against her forehead and got up. "You'll have to excuse me," she said. "I'm not feeling very well."

Leaving the guests to chatter among themselves, Corey and I followed Grandmother inside. She stopped in the kitchen and asked Mrs. Brewster to call Tracy. "These folks will be staying until next week's group arrives," she said. "I could really use some help, and I'm sure you could, too."

"I'll do my best to talk her into coming," Mrs. Brewster said. "Too bad she's such a nervous nellie." She looked at Grandmother closely. "If you don't mind my saying so, Mrs. Donovan, you don't look too good."

"I don't feel too good, either," Grandmother admitted. "When your world view changes overnight, it's bound to leave you a little shaken."

"I reckon so." Mrs. Brewster's eyes shifted to Corey and me. "See what your pranks have led to? Misery for everybody."

"That's not fair," Corey began, but Grandmother silenced her with a shake of her head.

"Hush, Corey," she said wearily. "I'm going to my room to read." She held up *Bleak House*, a thick novel by Charles Dickens. "The odious Mr. Tulkinghorn has just put poor Lady Dedlock in a terrible position, and I'm anxious about her."

Corey and I started to follow Grandmother into her apartment, but Mrs. Brewster stopped us. "Find that account book," she said, "and get this business done with. It's hard on your poor grandmother."

"It's hard on us, too," Corey said.

"Well, don't expect any sympathy from me." Finished with us, Mrs. Brewster picked up a scouring pad and attacked a blackened pot. "I sure wish Tracy was here," she muttered.

Before we left the kitchen, I glanced at the clock. Seven thirty-five. Four hours and twenty-five minutes to go until midnight.

To pass the time, Corey and I tried to play chess, but we couldn't concentrate. We set up Monopoly, Scrabble, and Clue but were unable to finish a game before our minds wandered to the burial ground. We took turns reading to each other from a collection of Edgar Allan Poe stories we'd found in the library, but considering what lay ahead, they were too scary.

At ten o'clock we sneaked into the kitchen and ate almost half a gallon of chocolate-chip ice cream. Back in my room, Corey suggested a game of hangman. Deciding that was a bad idea, we started working a crossword together. As we puzzled over a five-letter word, third letter "T," meaning "beyond the fringe," the grandfather clock chimed eleven forty-five.

"Oh, no," Corey whispered. "It's time."

As silently as our shaking legs could carry us, we sneaked through the kitchen and outside. High in the sky, the man in the moon looked down, his sad face slightly askew, and watched us run across the lawn. Dark on the silver grass, our shadows raced ahead of us.

We plunged into the bushes and battled our way through the brambles to the burial ground. The bad ones sat in their favorite tree, obviously waiting for us.

"Land sakes," Caleb muttered. "I'd forgotten how much noise the living make."

"It's those galumptious big shoes they wear." Seth swung his feet, bare as usual. "They're fit for elephants, they are."

I looked down at my thick-soled running shoes. They didn't look galumptious to me. But shoes were hardly the issue tonight.

Soundlessly, the bad ones dropped from the tree and joined us. "You're late," Ira said. "According to my reckoning, it's one minute past midnight."

"We had to find two more shovels," I said. "We left the others in the grove."

"And we almost forgot this." Corey held up a battery-operated lantern.

"Well, we'd best get busy." Caleb led us through the underbrush to Miss Ada's burial place. Corey switched on the lantern and set it on the ground. She looked surprisingly calm, but my heart was hammering so hard it shook my chest, and my hands were clammy with fear.

Cautiously, I poked at the dirt with my shovel.

"You got to work faster than that," Seth said. "Or we'll be here for a month of Sundays."

"Won't digging wake her up?" Corey whispered.

"We *told* you she ain't here." Seth kicked at the dirt. "Don't you never listen?"

All of us looked at the grove. An owl called, but nothing stirred in the dark trees. What's to stop her from coming, I wondered.

Reluctantly, I put more muscle into my task. The ground was surprisingly soft, and my shovel bit into it easily. Corey started digging, too. Soon we'd dug down at least three feet without coming across anything. Despite the cool night air, we were both sweating.

"Here, let me try." Seth grabbed Corey's shovel and went to work. Caleb took mine, and Ira settled down on his haunches, his eyes fixed on the grove.

All around us, the shadow children romped and played. "You're it," one cried. "Catch me if you can," another called.

Suddenly, Seth dropped his shovel and jumped backward. "I hit something."

"A tree root, most likely," Caleb said in a low voice. "Or a rock."

Ira grabbed the lantern and held it over the hole. Held fast by roots, the corner of a box protruded from the earth.

"Her coffin," Ira whispered.

We drew back. There was no sound but the wind in the trees, yet we felt Miss Ada's presence out there in the dark.

"Don't make a sound," Ira whispered. "Don't say a word, just finish digging."

Seth thrust his shovel at me. "I done my part."

Caleb and I bent to our task. Cautiously, we cleaned the dirt from the coffin's top. The lantern's light illuminated a tarnished metal plate: HERE LIE THE MORTAL REMAINS OF MISS ADA JAGGS.

My knees turned to water. It was all I could do to stand there and watch Caleb push the side of his shovel under the lid.

Corey grabbed Caleb's arm to stop him from prying the lid off. "Suppose the book's not in there?"

"It has to be," he muttered.

As Caleb leaned back on the shovel's handle, Corey covered her face with her hands. "I don't want to see her," she whispered.

Neither did I, but I couldn't turn my eyes away. Hypnotized with dread, I watched Caleb lever the lid up with a hideous screeching sound of nails pulling out of wood. In the coffin's darkness, I saw a skull, tangles of hair, and rags of clothing. Cradled in the bones of Miss Ada's hands was a rusty iron box.

Caleb reached down, grabbed the box, and handed it to me. "Take this back to the inn. Write down the names and numbers of the dead, so you can make proper tombstones for us all."

Seth and Ira closed the coffin lid, picked up the shovels, and began tossing dirt back into the grave. I wanted to help, but Caleb looked at the grove fearfully and shook his head. "Get out of here," he whispered. "Before she comes."

Leaving the bad ones to refill Miss Ada's grave, Corey and I ran across the lawn. The box was heavy and smelled of damp earth. It was slippery and awkward to hold. At any moment, I expected to hear Miss Ada's voice or feel her bony hand clutch my arm, my shoulder, my shirt. The harder I ran, the slower I seemed to move.

But, at last, Corey and I were at the inn's back door, fumbling with the knob, trying to be quiet but desperate to get inside. Fortunately, Grandmother was a sound sleeper, and we managed to get back to my room without waking her. I put the box on the floor. With a twist of my wrist, I broke the rusty padlock and lifted the lid.

The account book's leather cover was damp and stained

with mold. I picked it up, hating the rotten feel of it in my hands, and opened it.

Miss Ada had recorded the names of sixty-seven people, their ages, the dates they died, and the number assigned to them. Her old-fashioned handwriting slanted neatly to the right, and each letter was perfectly formed.

I opened my notebook and picked up a pen. Slowly and carefully, I copied the sixty-seven names, their ages, death dates, and burial numbers.

By the time I was finished, it was after three A.M., and Corey had fallen asleep on my bed. Too tired to worry about Miss Ada or anything else, I lay down on the rug and fell fast asleep.

18

In the morning, Corey and I carried the account book to the dining room. Grandmother was already seated at the table, drinking coffee and reading the morning paper. Mrs. Brewster was putting fresh flowers in little vases. The sun slanted in through the open French doors, bringing with it the sound of Mr. Brewster's riding mower and the sweet smell of cut grass.

It was hard to believe, but in this very room, Miss Ada and her brother had once eaten their fancy meals while the poor starved. The lawn Mr. Brewster mowed had been fields where men labored from dawn to dusk. People had died in what was now the carriage house.

I laid the account book in front of Grandmother. She set down her cup and stared at the soiled leather cover. "Where did you find this?"

"The bad ones told us where to look," I said, unwilling to tell her exactly where it had been hidden. "It has all the names and numbers, so we can make proper stones for the graves."

"Sixty-seven people are buried here," Corey put in.

"That many?" Grandmother opened the book and ran her finger down the list of names. "How awful."

"Miss Ada recorded the money they got from the county and how they spent it," Corey said. "Hardly any of it went to the poor people. They used it for themselves."

Grandmother looked at the accounts and shook her head. "Shameful, absolutely shameful."

Mrs. Brewster hovered at Grandmother's shoulder, scowling at the book. "The worst of it is, nothing's changed. All you have to do is look around at the rich people getting fat on the poor. Even the government ain't above it."

With a sigh, Grandmother closed the book and pushed it aside. "The county historical society will be interested in this."

Mrs. Brewster took our breakfast order. "When will you see to the headstones?" she asked Grandmother.

"The sooner the better." Grandmother turned to us. "I suggest we visit a stone mason in Barre today."

A few hours later, Grandmother led us into the office of Daniel Greene and Sons, Ltd. After a brief conversation with Mr. Greene Jr., Grandmother practically went into shock at the cost of purchasing sixty-seven gravestones.

"There's a less expensive option," Mr. Greene told us. "We could chisel all the names and numbers on one large stone at a savings of . . . "

He did some quick figuring on his calculator and came up with a price Grandmother could afford. "I'm willing to reduce my profit," he said, "because of the historical significance of what you're doing. There's many a name on this list whose descendants live here still. They deserve to know where their ancestors are buried."

Leading us outside, Mr. Greene showed us a number of precut stones and we chose a big pale pink marble slab. After more discussion, he promised the memorial would be ready as soon as possible.

Before we went back to the inn, we stopped at the historical society and asked to see Mrs. Bernice Leonard, the head archivist. She accepted Miss Ada's account book with gratitude.

"My great-great grandfather died at that farm," she said softly. "And so did his wife and some of his children. Their surname was Perkins. Are they among those in your book?"

Corey and I stared at the woman, gray haired and small, rosy faced, her hands clasping the unopened book. She had eyes as blue as Caleb's. And that dimple in her left cheek. It was as if something of Caleb lived still, his eyes and his dimple passing down and down and down from one Perkins to another.

"Abraham and Sarah Perkins." Grandmother opened the book and pointed to their names. "And their children, Matty and Caleb."

Mrs. Leonard touched the names. "I'm descended from their oldest son, Jonathon. He wasn't sent to the poor farm because he was indentured to a blacksmith." With a smile, she shook Grandmother's hand. "Thank you for bringing this to me."

"Thank Corey and Travis," Grandmother said. "They're the ones who found the book."

We left Mrs. Leonard turning the pages of the book and got into the truck, hot inside from sitting in the summer sun.

"I wish we could tell Mrs. Leonard about Caleb," Corey said.

"I don't think that would be a good idea," Grandmother said.

"Why not?"

Grandmother eased out of her parking space and headed south on Route 12. "I'd rather keep the ghosts secret," she said. "If word gets out, we'll have people like Chester Coakley banging on the door. Believe me, I don't want any more ghost hunters at the inn—no matter how many rooms they take."

That evening after dinner, the shadow children drifted through my window and filled the room with their familiar whispers and giggles. A few moments later, Corey arrived with Seth, Caleb, and Ira trailing behind her.

"Did Granny order the stones?" Seth asked me.

"Separate headstones turned out to be *really* expensive," Corey said in a low voice, looking ashamed.

"So there's going to one big pink stone with all the names and dates and numbers on it," I finished for her.

Surrounded by the shadow children, they whispered together for moment.

"That will do," Caleb said, "though we would have liked to have our own stones."

"I was hoping for a lamb," Seth said. "Or an angel."

"What of the account book?" Ira asked. "Did you put it somewhere safe?"

"We gave it to Mrs. Leonard at the county historical society," I said.

"She says she'll see it gets published, so everybody can read the truth about the poor farm."

"A fact simily," Corey added.

"*Facsimile*," I corrected her. "An exact copy of the original."

"Whatever." Corey shrugged.

"Mrs. Leonard is descended from your brother Jonathon," I told Caleb.

"And she's got your dimple," Corey added.

Caleb touched his cheek in wonder. "So Jonathon lived and got married and had a family? That's grand, that is."

"How about me?" Seth asked. "Is she kin to me, too?"

"The Brewsters are your kin," Ira reminded Seth.

Seth shrugged. "Yes, but the society lady sounds more highfalutin than my grumpy old auntie."

Corey yawned then, a big one without even covering her mouth, and rubbed her eyes.

"We didn't get much sleep last night," I reminded the bad ones.

At the same moment, the shadow children began whispering to each other. "Time to go," they whispered, "time to rest."

Caleb watched them drift along the wall toward the window and slip outside. "We'd better go, too," he said.

"Good luck with the third thing," Ira whispered.

In a snap of the fingers, the three boys were gone. A strange stillness lingered in the room, and the air felt charged the way it does before a thunderstorm.

"Wait." I ran to the window and peered out. The moon-white lawn was empty, the night silent. "Are you coming back? Will we see you again?"

There was no answer, just a stirring of leaves in the grove—and that odd silence.

Corey joined me at the window, standing so close her

shoulder touched my arm. I could feel her trembling. *"Good luck with the third thing,"* she whispered, echoing Ira's words.

"The third thing." I stared at my sister. "The account book, the tombstone, . . . and Miss Ada."

Suddenly, a breeze sprang up, and the curtains blew inward, brushing my face and my arms. They felt cold and damp, but when I tried to push them away, they clung to me, twisting around my body, trapping me.

"Give me my book," a voice hissed in my ear. "The one you stole from my grave."

19

It wasn't the curtains that trapped me. It was Miss
Ada's dress. Shaking with fear, I staggered backward,
trying to free myself, but the more I struggled, the
tighter the dress wrapped around me.

Nearby, Corey cried out in fear. I felt her lunging,
twisting, turning, but she couldn't escape, either.

Miss Ada's bony hands clutched us, numbing us with
cold, weakening our arms and legs. Limp with fear, we
gave up and stumbled against her. If she hadn't held us so
tightly, we would have fallen to the floor at her feet.
Released from the tatters of her dress, we stared into her
face, little more than a skull, its eyes as dark as the grave.

"My book," she said. "Give me my book."

"We don't have it," I whispered.

Miss Ada's eyes glowed with hatred. "Wicked children,
I saw you take it."

"It's—it's not here," Corey stammered.

"We gave it to the historical society," I added.

Miss Ada seemed to grow taller. Angrier. "You had no
right to do that! It was my book." She shook us. "You will
be punished for this."

Despite my terror, I managed to say, "You can't hurt us,
you're dead, and we're . . ." My voice cracked and
broke. I couldn't go on, not with her standing there, smiling a smile I wished I hadn't seen.

Keeping her grip on us, Miss Ada drew us close, closer yet, so close that all we saw was her eyes. It was as if the rest of the world had vanished. Nothing existed except Miss Ada's eyes. In their darkness, I saw every shameful thing I'd ever done—mistakes I'd made, mean things I'd done, people I'd hurt. I saw things I'd wanted but not gotten, things I'd lost. I saw my failures, my sorrows, my tears. I saw myself as Miss Ada wanted me to—a loathsome boy, despicable, unloved, pitiful and weak, stupid and selfish.

The smell of death filled my nostrils, the cold of the grave chilled me to the bone.

Beside me, Corey wept. "Stop," she sobbed. "Stop, please stop."

Miss Ada straightened up and sneered down at us. "Do you still believe the dead cannot hurt the living?"

Corey and I stared at her, speechless with misery and fear.

"Consider the years I've lain in the grave," she went on in a low voice, "learning the ways of darkness, strengthening myself, seeking vengeance."

"We're sorry," Corey whispered. "We didn't mean any harm. It was just a game, a prank. If you let us go, we'll never—"

"Hush!" Miss Ada shook Corey so hard she cried out with pain. "Your apologies and promises mean nothing to me. You mocked me, dug up my grave, stole my account book, exposed my secrets, collaborated with my enemies. You must be punished!"

With a terrifying strength, she yanked us through the open window and into the night. Unable to keep up, we stumbled behind her, arms aching, too weak to break away from her. The grove lay ahead, a black blot on the lawn.

"What are you going to do to us?" Corey whimpered.

"What does it matter?" Miss Ada pulled us into the grove. "You are worthless. You have nothing to live for."

"Nothing to live for, nothing to live for. Nothing, nothing, nothing. " The word spread out around us like fog, dark and cold, obscuring everything. It was true. I was worthless. No one loved me, no one cared. If I died, no one would miss me.

"Nothing, nothing, nothing. " The word was in the wind, in the grass, in the leaves, in the song the crickets sang.

I stopped struggling. *"Nothing, nothing, nothing."* I stopped fighting. *"Nothing, nothing, nothing. "* I didn't care what happened to me. *"Nothing, nothing, nothing."*

Nearby Corey struggled with Miss Ada. She struck at her, she kicked. "Do something, Travis!" she yelled. "Help me!"

But I just stood there watching my sister. Couldn't she see we *deserved* to be punished?

Keeping a tight grip on Corey, Miss Ada pointed upward. "See the noose up there? It's waiting for you. Climb to that branch, boy. *My* branch. The one *I* chose. Put the noose around your worthless neck and jump."

"No, Travis," Corey cried. "Don't listen to her—don't do it!"

Miss Ada shook my sister. "Be quiet," she said. "You'll be next."

While Corey sobbed, I began to climb slowly, like someone in a dream, hand over hand, from one branch to the next. All around me leaves rustled and sighed.

"Nothing, nothing, nothing." They brushed my face softly, tenderly. The tree swayed gently, lulling me. *"Nothing, nothing, nothing."*

The noose was just above my head. It turned slowly in the breeze. All I needed to do was climb to the next limb and slip it over my head. I boosted myself up carefully. I didn't want to fall. I had to do exactly as Miss Ada said. Follow her instructions. Atone for all the bad things I'd done.

As I reached for the noose, I looked down. Miss Ada stared up at me. Corey huddled at her feet. From this height, they were no bigger than the dolls in my sister's dollhouse.

"No," my sister cried. "Don't do it, Travis!"

I shook my head sadly "I must," I whispered to myself. "I must."

I reached out for the noose. The rope was hard, thick, old. It stank of mold. I tried to lift it over my head, but my hands shook so hard I dropped it. I watched it swing back and forth, back and forth, now in moonlight, now in shadow.

At the same moment, the breeze picked up and cool air struck my face. Suddenly, the darkness in my head began to lighten. Corey stood motionless below me, looking up, waiting. If I obeyed Miss Ada and put the noose around my neck, my sister would die, too.

"Do it!" Miss Ada screamed up at me. "Now!"

I shook my head, scared to defy her openly. The noose swayed, and I inched away from it, closer to the tree's solid trunk.

Miss Ada strode to the tree and began to climb. Her

ragged dress fluttered, and the moon splashed shadows across her bony face. "You will do as I say, boy!"

Safe on the ground, Corey watched. For her sake as well as mine, I forced myself to say, "No. I won't do it. I won't . . ."

"You will do as I say." Miss Ada stopped just below me and reached for the noose. "Take it," she said. "Accept your punishment like a man, not a whining boy."

"No," I whispered. But even as I spoke, I found myself weakening. Miss Ada was so near I could smell her earthy odor. Her hair swirled like a black cloud, blocking my view of Corey. I shut my eyes to keep from seeing her, but this close, her power over me began to grow again.

"Caleb," I whispered, "Seth, Ira—where are you?"

Just above my head, the leaves parted, and Caleb peered down at me. Ira and Seth crouched beside him. Over their heads, the shadow children made the branches sway.

"Climb up here!" Caleb whispered. "Don't let her get close."

Grabbing his hand, I scrambled higher into the tree. Miss Ada lunged for me, but even though my legs and arms shook, I managed to outclimb her.

"Come back here, you wicked boy," she cried, "and do as I say."

Nauseated, I held a branch tightly. Part of me still wanted to obey Miss Ada, but a stronger part of me wanted to save Corey. And myself.

"Caleb Perkins, is that you?" Miss Ada yelled.

Caleb poked his head out of the leaves. "Yes, ma'am, it's me, all right."

Ira and Seth peered down at Miss Ada. "We're here, too."

"Go back to the ground where you belong," Miss Ada cried. "The boy and girl are mine now. Do you hear me? Go!"

"We ain't going nowhere," Seth said.

"You have no power to punish the living," Ira put in, his eyes bigger and darker than ever.

Miss Ada reached for a higher limb and began hoisting herself closer to us. "Have you forgotten who I am," she hissed, "and what I can do?"

Caleb looked Miss Ada square in the eye. "Not a one of us has forgotten who you are or what you did to us and ours, but Ira and me have figured something out." He leaned a little closer to her. "Now that we're dead, all our suffering's over. You can't hurt us unless we let you."

"And you can't hurt Travis and Corey unless *they* let you," Ira said.

Caleb's hand held mine tightly, pulling me toward him, away from Miss Ada.

She glared up at the bad ones. "Whatever I did to you was your own fault," she said. "You defied me, you were never satisfied, never grateful. You *made* me punish you, you *made* me hurt you."

As Miss Ada ranted, the shadow children surged down from the treetop, laughing and mocking her. Limb by limb, branch by branch, they drove her down the tree.

"Old lady witch," they chanted, "lives in a ditch, counts every stitch, wants to be rich."

On the ground once more, Miss Ada shook her fist at the bad ones. "Everything I did was for your own good. You had to learn your place in the world!"

While she hurled anger and spite at them, the shadow

children dropped to the ground, barely visible in the moon-light, and circled the woman. One reached out and drew Corey into their midst. Ira, Caleb, Seth, and I scrambled down and joined them.

Holding hands, we whirled Miss Ada into a wild dance. Arms flailing, rags flying, hair tossing, she stumbled gracelessly as she reeled.

"Old lady witch," the shadow children sang, "go home to your ditch, scratch your itch, you'll never be rich!"

"Let me go," she cried. "Or—"

"Or what?" the shadow children jeered. "Your cane can't hurt none of us no more. We never eat, so you can't starve us. We don't feel the cold, so you can't freeze us."

"And you can't kill us," Seth shouted, "'cause we're already dead!"

With that, the shadow children retreated, still laughing. Corey dodged Miss Ada's outstretched hands, and the woman fell to the ground in a heap.

I put an arm around Corey and stared at the motion-less bundle of rags and bones. "Is she gone now?"

Seth shook his head. Poking Miss Ada with his toe, he said, "Best get up, old lady."

Slowly, the rags stirred. Miss Ada raised her head but remained where she'd fallen. The moon cast the noose's shadow across her face. Exhaustion hung from her shoulders like a heavy weight.

The three boys stood in a row and stared at her. Behind them, the shadow children watched her silently.

"How dare you look at me like that." Miss Ada stood up slowly and faced us, unsteady on her feet but as full of pride and anger as ever. Her hair blew around her face like dead grass, and her mouth opened like a dark hole. "Go back to your resting places."

The shadow children murmured to each other, filling the air with a sound like the rustling of leaves in an autumn breeze. But none of them moved. All kept their eyes on the woman.

"Why do you defy me?" she cried.

"Tell us you're sorry," Ira said, and the shadow children's voices grew louder. *"Yes, yes, yes, say you're sorry."*

"Sorry?" Miss Ada stared at the bad ones. *"Sorry?* You should apologize to *me*, not I to you!"

"It's the only way to save yourself," Ira said calmly.

"You'd better think of saving yourself," Miss Ada said in a voice deadly with scorn. "You deserved everything I did to you—and more!"

"Are you sure you're not sorry?" Ira asked.

"Not even a little bit?" Caleb added.

"How can the likes of her be sorry?" Seth asked. "She's got no heart. Never did. Never will. She'll be howling in the grove till the world ends."

"Old lady witch," the shadow children jeered again, "dead in her ditch, dead from the itch, never to be rich."

Ira stretched out his hand and touched the woman's shoulder. She jerked away, wincing as if he'd hurt her. "Don't you dare lay your filthy hands on me!"

"Say you're sorry for all you did to us," he pleaded, "not just us children but all the folks who lived and died on this farm."

"I told you, I have nothing to be sorry for." Miss Ada's bony hands clenched and unclenched the rags of her once fine silk dress. Her dull hair fell down her back, uncombed and matted with dirt and weeds. "I had a job to do, and I did it as I saw fit."

"If you weren't sorry," Caleb asked, "then why did you kill yourself?"

Seth started to say something, but Caleb put his hand over the little boy's mouth. "Shh," he whispered.

"Sorry had nothing to do with it," Miss Ada muttered. "My brother had taken our money and deserted me. I was ruined. Why live? They would have sent me to jail or . . . or . . . to a poor farm."

Seth jerked away from Caleb and laughed in Miss Ada's face. "I would've dearly loved to see you eating the stale bread you fed us!"

Miss Ada turned away to stare across the lawn at the inn. A man stood there, as still as death itself, barely visible in the darkness. "Cornelius," she whispered, "is that you?"

The man said nothing, but he raised his hand and gestured for her to join him.

Without knowing why, I cringed in fear. There was danger here. Corey sensed it, too, and drew closer to me. I could hear her breathing fast and shallow.

But Miss Ada gave a glad cry and took a step toward the shadowy figure.

To my surprise, Ira seized her arm. "Don't go—"

Furious, Miss Ada slapped his hand away. "Out of my way, boy. My brother has come for me at last."

"No!" Ira made another futile effort to stop her. "Look again!"

Caleb touched Ira's shoulder. "Let her go where she

must go. We can't give her eyes to see what she won't see."

"Let her go to the devil hisself!" Seth clapped his hands and laughed out loud.

The shadow children giggled. "Old lady witch," they chanted, "old lady witch, dead in the ditch."

Too scared to move or speak, Corey and I watched Miss Ada make her way across the lawn to the waiting man.

"I thought you'd left me to take all the blame," she called to him.

The figure in the shadows said nothing, but he held out his arms to her. At the same time, he grew taller and more menacing. In her eagerness to join him, Miss Ada didn't notice the change until she'd almost reached him.

Stopping a few feet away, she stared up into his face. "You're not Cornelius," she whispered, "You—you are—"

He reached out to embrace her, but with a desperate cry, Miss Ada turned and ran back to the grove. "I won't go with you. I won't!"

The man followed her silently. His shadow glided before him, engulfing everything in darkness.

To my horror, Miss Ada grabbed Corey. My sister screamed and struggled to escape, but her captor held her tight.

"Let her go!" I flung myself at the woman, but she dodged aside, leaving me holding nothing but a scrap of her dress.

"Take the girl!" Miss Ada thrust Corey toward the man. "Take her brother, too. Take all of them!" Her voice rose to a shriek. "But leave me be!"

"It's you I want, Ada." The man shoved Corey aside. "Not

her," he said in a low, chilling voice. "Not him. Not the others. Just you!"

"No, no, I implore you! Haven't I suffered enough?" Miss Ada wrung her hands in prayer. "Please, have mercy, don't take me!"

"Mercy?" The man laughed with scorn. "Mercy?"

"I didn't do anything," she whispered. "It was Cornelius. *He* made me do what I did. As for them"—she pointed at the bad ones—"if they'd done what I told them, if they'd obeyed me, if they'd respected me—"

"If." The man shook his head. "Such a little word to make such a big difference."

When he reached for her, Miss Ada tried again to escape, but no matter which way she moved, the man blocked her path. She wept, she cried, she begged, but he was implacable.

"Enough!" he shouted. With one swift move, he lifted her off her feet and into his arms. She kicked, she beat him with her fists, she cried for help, but he carried her out of the grove as if she were a child. Their shadows swept across the lawn, darkened the inn for a moment, and at last vanished into a darkness blacker than the night.

In the terrible silence that followed, I put my arm around Corey's trembling shoulders, glad for her human warmth. For a minute, maybe more, we stood as still as stones, staring at the empty lawn. As much as I'd feared and hated Miss Ada, I couldn't help pitying her.

Beside me, Ira whispered, "Poor soul."

Caleb sighed. "We tried to save her, but—"

"She weren't worth saving," Seth said. "Truth to tell, I'm glad she's gone where she's gone."

The shadow children echoed Seth. "Gone, gone, gone."

"But what happened to her?" Corey asked. "Who took her? Where did she go?"

"Don't fret yourself," Caleb said quietly. "It doesn't matter where she went or who took her."

"All you got to know is she ain't coming back," Seth said with a grin. "She's been exorcised but good."

"Soon we'll be gone, too," Ira said in his melancholy way.

"But not where she went," Seth added hastily.

"All we need now is that stone," Caleb said, "with our names and dates on it. Then we'll be free of this place."

Surrounded by the shadow children, the boys huddled together in the dark grove, their faces pale and weary of waiting.

"The stone will be ready soon," I promised—but I hoped not too soon. I wanted the bad ones to stay a while, even though I knew that they, too, had to go where they had to go.

20

A week or so after Miss Ada left Fox Hill, Corey and I were sitting on the patio, drinking lemonade and reading. The bad ones had gone off somewhere the way they often did now, saying nothing, just disappearing. Ira had told us it was getting wearisome to stay visible, so we supposed they were resting somewhere—maybe in the grove, maybe at the burial ground, maybe someplace we didn't even know about.

Suddenly, the *beep, beep, beep* of a truck backing up shattered the bird song. Corey and I dropped our books and ran to the front of the inn. With Grandmother watching from the porch, a flatbed truck maneuvered through a gap in the bushes bordering the poor-farm burial ground.

Tracy opened the screen door and poked her head out. She'd been back for a couple of days, but she was still a little jumpy. "What's that truck doing here?"

"It's bringing the headstone," Corey said. "For the burial ground."

Tracy looked at us, suddenly tense. "What burial ground?"

"Behind the barn," Grandmother said. "Corey and Travis discovered it. We thought we should memorialize the people laid to rest there."

Tracy closed the door and stared at us through the screen. "Does it have something to do with the ghosts?"

"It's just an old burial ground, Tracy," Grandmother said patiently. "The ghosts are gone now. I told you it was a hoax."

She bit her lip. "I'd better go make the beds," she said.

"Don't you want to see the men put up the stone?" I asked, thinking it might scare her and I could hold her hand or something.

"No," she said, "I have work to do."

Mrs. Brewster came up behind Tracy. "After you make the beds, please start the laundry. We're low on table linens."

"Yes, ma'am." Tracy disappeared, and Mrs. Brewster came outside to join us.

Followed by Mr. Brewster, we walked across the lawn to the burial ground. Unseen by the workmen, Caleb, Ira, and Seth waved to us from their favorite tree, and the shadow children flitted here and there among the graves.

It took the men a while to get the slab of marble off the truck and into place. The bad ones watched every move they made, coming so close to the men it's a wonder they weren't stepped on.

One of the man shivered. "This place gives me the creeps," he said. "Not that I believe in ghosts, but—" He broke off with a laugh.

"Tom, you been out in the sun too long," the other man said.

In the meantime, Seth picked a handful of daisies and dropped them by the stone.

The two men watched the flowers float down to earth. Neither one looked at the other. "Windy today," Tom said.

The shadow children gathered around the men and

began tossing flowers and giggling. "Pinchy, pinchy," they whispered.

The man named Tom swatted his leg. "Mosquitoes," he muttered. "Fierce, too."

The other slapped his neck. "Worse than usual. Must be those new ones from Africa or someplace."

Corey and I covered our mouths to hide our grins.

When Grandmother got out her checkbook, the two men were already in the truck, revving the engine.

"Don't worry about that now, ma'am," Tom said. "We'll tell Mr. Greene to send the bill." And off they went, leaving a cloud of dust and the smell of gasoline behind.

"You rascals." Grandmother frowned up into the maple tree. "You scared those men off."

"It was purely an accident on my part," Seth said. "But that bunch"—he pointed at the shadow children—"they done it a-purpose."

Grandmother's frown vanished and she laughed. "Is the memorial satisfactory?"

Seth grinned. "Yes, ma'am, Granny. That's a mighty fine hunk of marble."

Grandmother looked at Caleb and Ira.

"We got what we wanted," Ira said, "all the names and dates and numbers. Everything spelled proper, too." His fingers brushed his and his family's names.

"I reckon we're at peace at last," Caleb added, with a sigh of pure contentment.

While the bad ones thanked us, the shadow children swarmed over the big stone, dappling it with patches of darkness, finding their names and the names of their friends and relatives.

"Here I am—Samuel Greene!" one called out. "And here's my ma and pa and my two little brothers, all of us dead on the same day of typhus."

"And here's me—Edward Bellows—and my ma and pa, taken by the same wicked typhus."

"It was a hard life we lived," Seth said, "but it was over way too soon."

Mr. Brewster gazed at him. "We won't know what to do when you're gone. Martha and me been watching you for more than forty year now."

"Tell your ma the Brewsters kept their word to look after you, generation to generation," Mrs. Brewster said.

"Yes, Auntie." Seth suffered the woman to hug him. "I'll tell all you done, and they'll be right pleased."

"When will you be leaving us?" Grandmother asked.

"We'll wait till dark," Caleb said.

"So the stars can guide us," Ira added.

All this time, my sister and I had just stood there, trying not to cry and failing miserably. "We'll miss you so much," Corey said.

"Why, we'll miss you, too," Caleb said. "You've been good friends to us. All of you—"

"Even Granny," Seth put in. "She weren't keen on us at the start, but she come round real good at the end."

Grandmother smiled and tried to hide her tears. "Well, it's been a strange experience for me, a person who didn't believe in ghosts and never expected to see any—let alone miss them when they left."

"Wasn't it Shakespeare who said, 'There are more things in heaven and earth, Horatio, than are dreamt of in your philosophy'?" Ira asked.

Caleb nodded. "*Hamlet*, act one. Something else we memorized in our school days before we set foot in this cursed place."

"Little did we think then that we'd soon be ghosts ourselves," Ira said in his melancholy way, "haunting the place we died, looking for justice, just like Hamlet's father."

Seth clapped him on the back. "But we got justice at last, didn't we?"

"And we got rid of Miss Ada," Caleb said.

Seth grinned. "So you needn't be gloomy no more, Ira."

Ira smiled, but the sadness in his eyes was still there.

"Now," Caleb said, "it's time to take a last look at this place, boys."

Without inviting us to join them, the bad ones vanished, and we were left to admire the new stone and its sixty-seven names.

Late that night, long after the guests had gone to bed, we sat on the porch, waiting to say goodbye to the bad ones. When they finally showed up, they blended in with the shadow children, as if they'd lost the strength to become visible.

"Thank you once more for all you did for us," Caleb said.

Ira carefully placed an old pot in Grandmother's hands. "It's the money Mr. Jaggs aimed to steal from the poor farm."

Grandmother opened the pot. "Gold coins," she whispered.

"Two hundred and twenty five-dollar pieces," Ira said.

"You're rich, Granny!" Seth crowed.

Grandmother lifted a handful of coins and let them run through her fingers, *clinkety-clink*. "I'll see this goes to a good cause," she said. "Habitat for Humanity, maybe, or Oxfam."

"Surely you'll keep it for yourself," Seth said.

Grandmother smiled at him. "That wouldn't be right, Seth. This money was stolen from the poor, and it must go back to the poor."

"Granny's right." Ira put his arm around Seth.

Seth sighed. "Maybe you could keep just one for yourself—to remember us by."

Grandmother's smile widened. "Oh, I don't think there's any danger of my forgetting you."

They gathered around us then and said their goodbyes. The shadow children clung like cobwebs to our arms and legs, whispering and giggling.

Then, the lovely bad ones drifted away across the lawn like milkweed blown by the wind. They rose slowly into the sky, as if they were climbing stairs only they could see. Higher and higher they went, shrinking until they were no more than dots of light indistinguishable from the stars.

Long after they'd disappeared, we sat quietly and stared at the sky, trying to imagine where they had gone. Was it a long journey? Would they remember us when they got there?

With a sigh, Mr. Brewster got to his feet and reached down for his wife's hand. "Come on, old girl. Tomorrow's coming soon. You got breakfast to cook, and I got chores to do."

Grandmother put her arms around Corey's and my shoulders and hugged us close to her side. "It already seems like a dream."

"But it wasn't," I said.

"It was totally real," Corey agreed.

More real than we'd ever imagined the night Corey had run across the lawn in her ghost costume. We'd sure learned a lot about ghosts since then—maybe even more than was good for us.

Suddenly, Grandmother said, "Look!"

High above the earth, a shooting star streaked across the sky.

We gazed at each other, our faces solemn. No one said it, but I knew we were all thinking the same thing. The lovely bad ones were home at last.

About the Author

MARY DOWNING HAHN, a former children's librarian, is the award-winning author of many popular ghost stories, including *Deep and Dark and Dangerous* and *The Old Willis Place*. An avid reader, traveler, and all-around arts lover, Ms. Hahn lives in Columbia, Maryland, with her two cats, Oscar and Rufus.